ROBERT J HARRIS

LEONARDO AND THE DEATH MACHINE

HarperCollins *Children's Books*

First published in Great Britain by HarperCollins *Children's Books* 2005
HarperCollins *Children's Books* is a division of HarperCollins *Publishers* Ltd
77-85 Fulham Palace Road, Hammersmith, London, W6 8JB

www.harpercollinschildrensbooks.co.uk

1 3 5 7 9 8 6 4 2

Map illustration by Fiona Land

ISBN 0 00 719423 4

Printed and bound in Great Britain by
Clays Ltd, St Ives plc

For Debby, who gave me my wings.

The Prato
N
W
E
S
Med
Hous
Sandro's House
River Arno
Ponte Vecch
Santo Spirito
Pitti Palace

Leonardo and the Death Machine

Titles by Jane Yolen and Robert J Harris

Jason and the Gorgon's Blood

Odysseus and the Serpent Maze

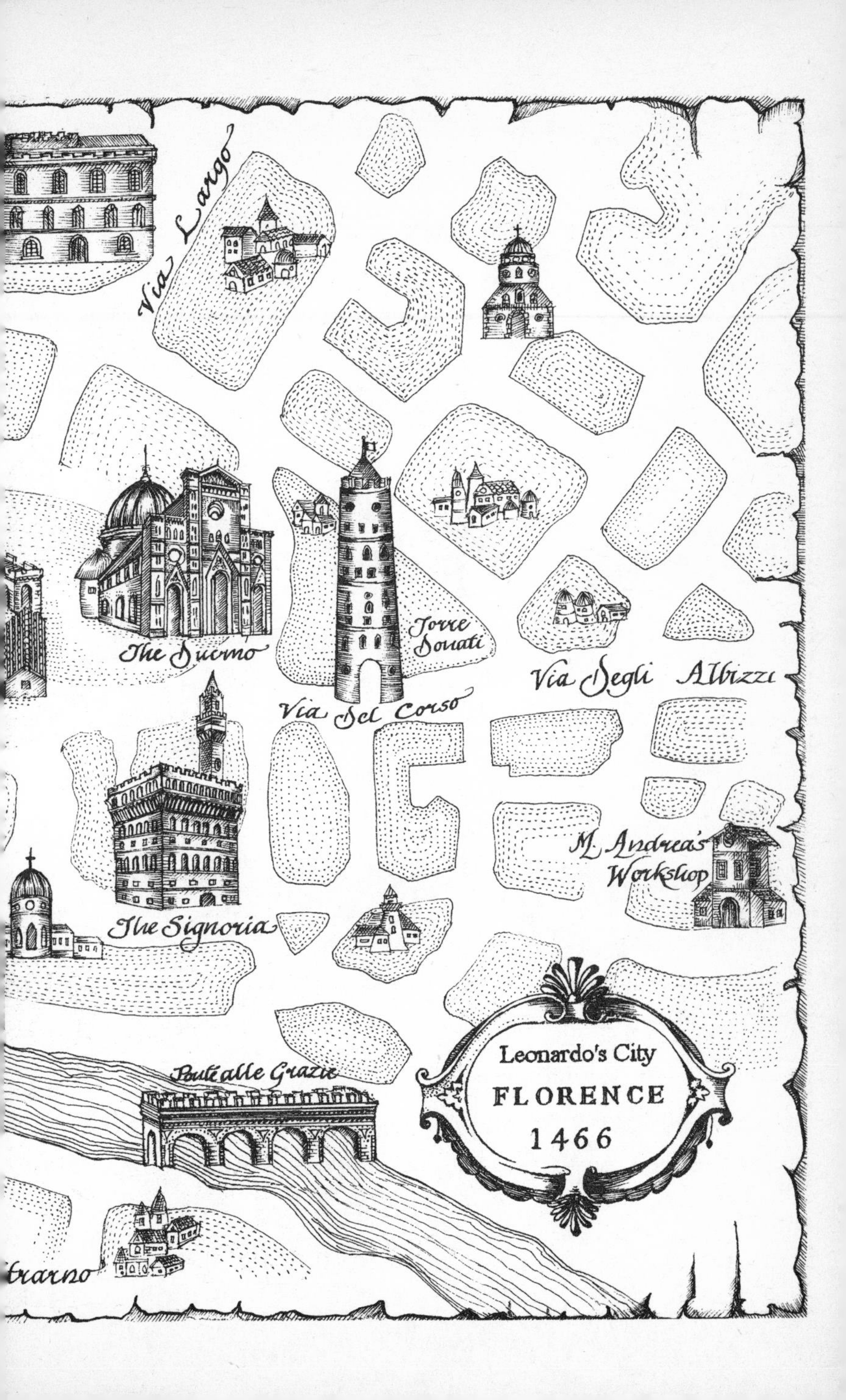

Via Largo
The Duomo
Torre Donati
Via Del Corso
Via Degli Albizzi
The Signoria
M. Andrea's Workshop
Leonardo's City
FLORENCE
1466
Ponte alle Grazie
trarno

1

Fishbones and Fire

"One – two – three," Leonardo muttered, counting each stroke of the mallet. The third hit drove the nail flat into the wood, fixing another stretch of canvas on to the frame.

Only two more nails to go. "One" – thud – "two" – thud – "three" – thud.

There were twenty nails in all and at least three knocks were required to bash each one in. If he didn't hit the nail just right, it would bend in half. When that happened, the bent nail had to be worked loose and tossed away so that a new one could be hammered in its place.

"Make sure you knock those nails in straight, country boy,

otherwise you'll tear the canvas," warned Nicolo. He was finishing a painting of a laughing woman, using a bust made by their master as a model. At seventeen he was the senior apprentice in the workshop. The master, Andrea del Verrocchio, was away at a meeting with the members of the Signoria, the ruling council of Florence, leaving Nicolo in charge.

"No need to worry about that," said Leonardo. "This is the last one."

Mentally, he painted the older boy's face in miniature on the head of the final nail and brought the mallet down with a vengeful whack. Leonardo stared in amazement at the result and grinned. For the first time he had driven the nail right into the wood with a single blow. He would have to remember that trick.

He stood up to admire his handiwork and caught a whiff of rotten fish. The smell stung his nostrils and made his stomach lurch.

"Horrible, isn't it?" said skinny little Gabriello. He was stirring fishbones around in an iron pot over a raised brick fire pit. This melted them into a paste that was spread over the canvas before any paint was applied.

"Still, it could be worse," the little apprentice added. "We could be using calf hooves again and they *really* stink."

"Some things smell even worse than that," said Leonardo with a sidelong glance at Nicolo.

Gabriello chuckled, then coughed as the fishy fumes got into his throat. The senior apprentice did not notice the insult. He was too busy painting the last few locks of the woman's hair, his tongue stuck into his cheek in concentration.

Leonardo lifted the frame up off the straw-covered floor and leaned it carefully against one of the worktables. He nodded in satisfaction. The frame was firmly constructed, the canvas straight and taut. When Maestro Andrea came to inspect it, he would be pleased.

A gust of wind from the open window sent a puff of acrid dust up his nose. Leonardo turned away quickly so that his sneeze missed the canvas, then waved his hands about to clear the air.

The dust came from the corner of the room where Vanni and Giorgio were standing over a slab of porphyry, grinding brightly coloured minerals with their mortars. This produced a fine powder which would be mixed with egg to make paints. They were chatting together and occasionally breaking into song, their voices rising raucously above the rumble of passing carts and the yells of pedlars hawking their wares in the street outside.

"Pipe down and pay attention to what you're doing!" Nicolo barked at them. "You're spreading that dust all over the room."

Leonardo pulled out his kerchief and blew his nose. He had thought that when his father brought him to Florence to be a pupil in the workshop of a great artist, he would be leaving behind the dirt and stench of the farmyard. But there was just as much dirt here and the stench was even worse. When Maestro Andrea was sculpting a statue, the dust hung so thick in the air it was like a chalky fog. And always there was the stink of fishbones, eggs, charcoal, turpentine and all the other unglamorous materials of the artist's trade.

Tucking his kerchief back into his sleeve, Leonardo went to the corner where his own paintings and sketches were stored. Reaching into the midst of them, he pulled out his latest work, one which Maestro Andrea had not assigned him. As he examined the object, Nicolo's voice boomed out behind him.

"There! It is done!"

From his grandiose tone you would have thought he had just fitted the last brick into the great dome of the cathedral instead of completing a routine exercise.

Nicolo beckoned Vanni and Giorgio over to admire his

'masterpiece'. They gladly left their grinding materials behind and hurried over to examine the canvas, brushing the mineral dust from their aprons.

"It's very good, Nicolo," said Vanni, knowing exactly what he was supposed to say.

"Yes, it's very good," Giorgio echoed automatically.

Leonardo strolled over and eyed the finished picture. All the life and animation of Maestro Andrea's sculpture had been lost in Nicolo's painting. It was as if he had strained the meat and vegetables out of a rich stew and reduced it to a thin, unappetising gruel.

"So what do you think, Leonardo da Vinci?" Nicolo asked. The stern challenge in his voice made it clear exactly how Leonardo was supposed to answer. But Leonardo had taken enough insults from Nicolo that he wasn't going to let slip this chance to hit back.

"I think that if a corpse ever wants its portrait painted, you'll be the man for the job," he replied. Gabriello slapped a hand over his mouth to stifle a laugh. Nicolo growled and raised his fist.

Leonardo took a step back but did not flinch. He was three years younger than the senior apprentice but equal in both height and strength. If Nicolo wanted a fight, he was ready – and eager – to oblige. But Maestro Andrea had made it clear that anyone caught fighting in the workshop would immediately find himself out on the street without a *denaro* to his name.

The same thought was evidently in Nicolo's mind. He lowered his fist, though his face was still ruddy with anger. "You may dress up like the son of a rich man," he sneered, "but you still have the taste of a farm boy."

Leonardo winced. He was proud of the blue velvet tunic and scarlet hose he wore under his apron, even though he knew some of the other apprentices sniggered at his finery.

"At least I have some taste," he retorted. He waved at the painting. "This isn't art. This is murder."

Nicolo's eyes flashed with rage. "It is more than a clumsy left-hander like you could ever do!" Then he spotted what was in Leonardo's hand and snatched the wooden object from the younger boy's grasp. "What's this? Some sort of toy?"

"Give that back!" cried Leonardo hotly. He made a grab that Nicolo easily avoided. The senior apprentice waved his prize in the air so that everyone could see it.

It was a wooden cylinder, small enough to fit into a man's hand, with a piece of cord dangling from a hole in the side. There was another hole in the top into which a wooden spindle had been fitted. From the end of the spindle, four thin wooden blades spread out in different directions like the petals of a flower.

"Is that what you've been doing in that corner all this time?" asked Vanni.

"It looks like a little windmill," said Giorgio, "except the vanes are on top instead of on the side."

"Is that what it is, country boy?" Nicolo asked. "A toy windmill to remind you of life on the farm?"

"No, not at all," said Leonardo, so annoyed he could hardly speak.

"Maybe it's a baby's rattle." Nicolo shook the wooden device by his ear, but it made no sound. Leonardo was tempted to make another grab but he was afraid of damaging his creation.

"I give up, Leonardo," smirked Nicolo. "What does it do?"

Leonardo glared at him. "It flies."

"Flies?" The answer was so incredible it wiped the sneer from Nicolo's face.

"A merchant from Padua was selling one like it in the market," Leonardo explained. "He said it came from Cathay and he wanted five florins for it."

Vanni let out a low whistle. It was a sum beyond the imagination of apprentices like themselves.

"But for a few *denari* he let me examine it to see how it worked."

"And then you made your own," said Gabriello admiringly.

"Yes, I finished carving the four blades last night."

"And you think it will fly?" snorted Nicolo. "You've gone mad, country boy. The smell of turps has rotted your brain."

"Here, I'll show you," Leonardo offered, reaching for the device.

Nicolo yanked it out of reach. "Not so fast," he said. "We have to make sure there's no trickery here. How does it work?"

Leonardo gritted his teeth and reined in his temper. Ever since he had arrived at the workshop three months before, Nicolo had been goading him, mimicking the country accent he had been working so hard to erase, sneering at his drawings and telling him his hands were better suited to the plough than the brush and palette.

"There's a screw inside and the stick with the vanes on top is fitted into that," Leonardo explained slowly and carefully. "When you pull the string, the screw turns and sets the vanes spinning."

"That's it?" Nicolo asked.

Leonardo nodded. Grinning, Nicolo took a tight grip on the cord and prepared to pull.

"No, let me do it!" yelled Leonardo.

It was too late. Nicolo jerked his elbow back so hard the string snapped off. No one noticed that. What they noticed was the flying. Its blades a spinning blur, the spindle shot into the air, drawing gasps of astonishment from the apprentices.

"It's sorcery!" Gabriello squeaked as the flying device came twirling towards him. It hovered for a second over the metal grille of the fire pit. Then – to Leonardo's horror – it dropped.

Gabriello leapt away with a squeal of panic. Leonardo lunged for the device as it fell between the bars of the grille.

Too late again. There was a clang and a crash and a screech from Vanni.

Leonardo had knocked the gooey mess of bubbling fishbones on to the fire. Gobs of it ignited and burst into the air like shooting stars. They rained down on the floor and in an instant the straw covering burst into flames.

Gabriello and the other apprentices stampeded for the door.

"You stupid bumpkin!" Nicolo howled at Leonardo. "You've set the house on fire!"

2

The Debt Collector

Leonardo clenched his fists and fought down his panic. What was he to do? In a few moments the fire could spread out of control. The only firefighters in the city were some volunteers from the stonemasons' guild, but there was no time to summon them.

Then he remembered how his Uncle Francesco had stopped a fire that sprang up in the barn when one of the cows kicked over a lantern. Looking quickly around, he snatched the dust covering from one of Maestro Andrea's paintings. He hurled it over the fire and flung his own body on top of it to smother the flames.

He could feel the heat beneath him and smell the charred straw. Leonardo screwed his eyes tight shut and he held his breath, half expecting to be incinerated. That was still preferable to the humiliation of seeing the workshop destroyed through his clumsiness.

An excited babble of voices prompted him to open his eyes. Gabriello was leaning over him. "I think the fire's out," he said.

The other apprentices gathered around, nervously giggling and elbowing each other. Their faces were still white with shock. Leonardo propped himself up on one elbow, looking around for Nicolo.

"You saw, didn't you?" he challenged. "You saw it fly."

"I saw a stick jump into the air and fall into the fire," Nicolo replied. He shook his head. "Not very impressive."

Nicolo still had the other part of the flying device in his hand and now he flung it away contemptuously. It clattered across the floor and rolled out of sight under a table.

A rage hotter than any fire welled up inside Leonardo's breast. He would knock that smirk off Nicolo's face, no matter what the consequences.

He jumped to his feet. But before he could swing a punch, the door banged open.

Maestro Andrea del Verrocchio marched in, a dozen

rolls of parchment tucked under one arm and a heavy leather satchel slung over the other. He strode briskly across the room towards his study without even looking at his apprentices.

"Leonardo da Vinci!" he called as he vanished through the doorway.

Leonardo started guiltily. "Yes, Maestro?"

"Fetch me a pitcher of water! The rest of you, this is not a holy day. Get back to work!"

Nicolo snatched the scorched covering off the floor and stuffed it away out of sight under a workbench. Vanni and Giorgio gathered up the burnt straw and pitched it out of the window. Gabriello darted off to prepare a fresh pot of fishbones.

Leonardo rushed out of the back door to the pump and filled a pitcher with fresh water. When he got to the study, Maestro Andrea had laid down his scrolls and satchel and was studying some letters. Leonardo poured a cup of water and handed it to him.

"Don't leave," the maestro said as he lifted the cup to his lips. "I have something else for you to do."

As Maestro Andrea drank, Leonardo looked around at the drawings that littered the tables and the walls, studies of saints and angels, soldiers and animals.

With his round, pleasant face and stout belly, Andrea looked like a prosperous baker. In fact, he was one of the most brilliant and successful artists in Florence. He was so busy that he sometimes had to bring in other artists as his assistants. Recalling this, Leonardo had the exciting thought that perhaps the master was going to ask for his help in completing a major work.

Andrea gulped down the last of the water and smacked his thick lips. "Arguing terms with the members of the Signoria is thirsty work," he said. "Still, if our government want a new statue of St. Thomas for their chapel they will have to pay a decent price."

Leonardo tried to sound businesslike too. "I finished stretching the canvas, Maestro," he reported.

"I saw that when I came in," said Andrea, "just as I saw the overturned pot and the burnt straw and smelled the charred fishbones."

Leonardo was astonished. He could have sworn the master had not so much as glanced their way before entering his study. "There was an accident," he began apologetically.

Andrea raised a hand to silence him. "You are young men with high spirits and you will have your misadventures. As long as no one was hurt, there is no more to say."

"You said you had something for me to do," Leonardo reminded him.

"Yes, here it is," said Andrea. He presented the boy with a folded sheet of parchment sealed with a blob of wax.

"What's this?" Leonardo asked eagerly. "A sketch of the new work you've been commissioned to do? Would you like me to do the preliminary outlines?"

Maestro Andrea shook his head. "It's a bill for fourteen florins," he stated flatly.

"A bill?" Leonardo's heart plummeted. "Maestro, don't make me a debt collector. I came here to be an artist."

"Money is the lifeblood of art, Leonardo. If you haven't learned that by now you should go back to your father and be a notary like him."

The suggestion stung Leonardo like a hot needle. "No, I don't want to be like *him*. But I hoped…"

"You hoped what?" Andrea asked.

Leonardo raised his head to meet his master's eye. This was no time to be nervous and awkward. That would not earn his respect.

"I hoped you would have a proper piece of art for me to do, not a practice painting on used canvas or a wax model."

"What? Have you aged ten years overnight? Have the talents of the masters seeped into your soul while you slept?

To become an artist takes years and you have been here for only a few months."

"You do not become an artist by running errands, Maestro," Leonardo persisted.

Andrea peered down his snub nose at the boy. "I have told all of you many times that an artist begins his work by seeing and completes it by understanding. What are you going to see sitting around here? I'm giving you the chance to go out and find some inspiration. Now take this note to Maestro Silvestro's workshop."

"The one who borrowed that bronze from you last month?"

"The very same," Maestro Andrea confirmed. "He still hasn't replaced it, so I'll have the money instead."

"But it's in the Oltrarno," Leonardo complained, wrinkling his nose. This was the name given to the area of the city on the southern side of the River Arno. It was still more village than city and was notorious for its floods and outbreaks of plague.

"Very true," Andrea agreed dryly. "I am sure your beautiful clothes will bring a welcome dash of colour into the lives of the unhappy people who live there."

Leonardo straightened his tunic and flicked a spot of ash from his sleeve. "All the young gentlemen of Florence are dressing like this," he said defensively.

"All the *rich* young gentlemen of Florence," Maestro Andrea corrected him.

"There's nothing wrong with making a good impression."

"You are quite correct," said Andrea, waving him away dismissively. "Now go and make a good impression on Maestro Silvestro."

Leonardo returned to the workshop, taking off his smock as he headed for the door.

"Where are you going?" Nicolo demanded.

"I have an important commission from Maestro Andrea," Leonardo answered haughtily. "He wants me to exercise my eyes and my understanding."

Escaping from the workshop, Leonardo strode off down the Via dell'Agnolo, muttering resentfully to himself. After all his hard work his flying device was ruined, and now he was reduced to collecting debts. He very much doubted he would see anything to inspire him today.

In this year of 1466, Florence was the centre of trade and banking for all of Europe, and the bustle in the narrow streets bore witness to the city's importance. Wagons and carriages jostled alongside workers hurrying to and from the foundries and textile factories. Buildings rose up to three storeys high, with balconies jutting out of the top floors. Neighbours on opposite sides of the street could almost reach across and shake hands with each other.

As he approached the River Arno, Leonardo saw the flatboats heading downstream, carrying off their bolts of brightly coloured Florentine cloth to be transported to Spain, France, England and Germany. Other boats were bringing their cargo of untreated wool into the city to be washed, combed and dyed in the factories.

The city's oldest bridge, the Ponte Vecchio, loomed ahead, its honey-coloured stonework bathed in the glow of the hot August sunshine. Both sides of the bridge were lined with the shops of butchers, leatherworkers and blacksmiths. As Leonardo crossed over, a blacksmith tipped a bucket of ashes into the river, provoking a volley of curses from the boatmen passing below.

As soon as he entered the Oltrarno, Leonardo was reminded of his home village of Anchiano, many miles to the north. Washing was strung between the trees, chickens scratched at the doorsteps, and everywhere there was the smell of garlic and baking bread.

In stark contrast to the humble cottages was the huge stone palace Leonardo could see rearing up like a cliff face in the middle of the Oltrarno, with workers swarming all over its scaffolding. He knew from the gossip of his fellow apprentices that it belonged to Luca Pitti, an ageing politician who liked to think of himself as Florence's leading citizen. Even though the real power in the city lay in the hands of the Medici family, Pitti was determined to prove that he was every bit their equal, even if he went bankrupt in the process.

Leonardo turned right, away from the palace and towards the church of Santo Spirito. Silvestro's workshop was in one of the alleys behind the church, but Leonardo wasn't sure which one. He paused to sniff the air and immediately caught the pungent scent of cow dung, burnt ox-horn, and wet clay, all of which were used in the casting of bronze statues.

Following his nose he soon arrived at the shabby workshop of Silvestro. The shutters hung drunkenly from the windows and there were several tiles missing from the roof. Acrid smoke streamed from Silvestro's furnace and hung in a sullen, black cloud over the street. Finding the door ajar, Leonardo pushed it open and stepped inside.

A pair of surly apprentices in stained, threadbare smocks looked up as he entered. They were mixing up a supply of casting wax. One had a face covered in pimples while the other was twitching as though his clothes were filled with lice.

Proud of his own finery, Leonardo drew himself up in a dignified fashion and inquired, "Is Maestro Silvestro at home?"

The two apprentices turned to each other with dull, expressionless eyes. Leonardo was reminded of a pair of oxen in a field.

"He's in his private studio," grunted Pimple-face.

"And where would that be?" asked Leonardo.

The Twitcher tilted his head to indicate a stout door at the far end of the workshop.

With a curt nod of thanks, Leonardo moved on. Behind him he heard one of them mutter, "He must think he's an envoy from the Pope." The other apprentice sniggered.

Leonardo ignored them and cast his eyes over the room. The shelves along the wall held only a few jars of pigment and these were thickly caked with dust. Discarded bristles and splinters of wood littered the rush-covered floor.

As he raised his fist to rap on Silvestro's door, Leonardo was brought up short by a sudden outburst of angry voices from the room beyond. They were as furious as a couple of dogs fighting over a bone. Even muffled by the door their words were clearly audible.

"Today! You said today!" snarled the first voice, rough as sandstone.

"I said the components would be complete by today," the second voice boomed like a gusty wind. "I never said the construction would be complete, never!"

"I think you know what happens to men who cross me," rasped the first man.

"Save your threats for those you are paid to terrorise," the second man said. "All will be ready on schedule." Leonardo could hear the weakness underlying his confident words.

"Very well," the first voice grated. "But I will hold you to that at some cost if you should fail."

"Silvestro does not fail," the other retorted with renewed bravado. "He is only let down by lesser men. Do not worry, we will bring destruction down on the plain, eh?"

"Be sure of it," was the brusque response.

Leonardo had been leaning in closer and closer. When the door opened, his heart leapt into his mouth. He jumped aside as a fearsome individual in a dark green hood and cloak swept out of the room.

3

The Infernal Device

The stranger halted and fixed Leonardo with a hostile stare. The man's sallow face was all sharp angles with heavy brows and a slash of a mouth – as if it had been carved from flint by an impatient sculptor and left unfinished.

Leonardo felt himself being probed by the cold, grey eyes. He had the awful feeling that if the man suspected he had been listening at the door, his life would not be worth a single *denaro.*

The stranger's gaze moved down over Leonardo's garb, his expensive tunic and scarlet hose. A flicker of amusement curled his lips. *You are obviously no threat*, that thin smile seemed to say. *I don't need to waste any time on you.*

Without speaking, he turned and walked away. Leonardo felt insulted and relieved at the same time. Taking advantage of the open door, he stepped cautiously into Maestro Silvestro's chamber.

The artist was standing at the far end of the room with his broad back to the doorway. He was grumbling angrily to himself as he poured a cup of wine. He tossed the drink back in one swift draught, like a man throwing water over a blazing fire, and immediately refilled his cup.

"I'll skewer *him*, that cut-throat, if he talks to me like that again," Leonardo heard him growl.

He paused inside the doorway, uncertain what to do next. *See and understand*, Maestro Andrea had told him. He studied the artist in silence. He noted that Silvestro's once expensive clothes had been sewn up and patched many times over. That suggested he had once been a prosperous artist who had fallen on hard times. The fact that the clothes hung about his body in loose folds meant he had also grown thinner. Probably through guzzling jugs of wine in place of his meals, Leonardo guessed.

He peered around as Silvestro continued to mutter

bitterly into his cup. Immediately to his right stood the master's desk, its surface cluttered with coloured vials, lengths of decorative framing, and jars of powder and ink. Leonardo's eye was immediately drawn to a large sheet of paper that lay in the midst of the confusion. It was covered in drawings the like of which he had never seen before.

He took a furtive step closer to the desk. The page was crammed with intricate diagrams of notched wheels, pulleys, rods and weights, all fitted together into a complex mechanism.

Is this what the two men were arguing about? Leonardo wondered. *And if so, what is it?*

He had seen arrangements of cogs before, in the watermill on his family property at Anchiano, but nothing quite like this. Once he had even seen something similar inside an expensive clock that Maestro Andrea was embellishing for one of his clients. But this device was not exactly like that either.

What was it they had said about destruction?

He peered intently at the diagram, trying to piece together in his mind what would be the consequence of the weights moving, of the cogs turning one against the other. With one finger he began to follow the lines, tracing out the possible movements of the device. He was so absorbed in his study he was taken completely by surprise when a beefy hand clamped on to his shoulder.

"Who the devil are you?"

Maestro Silvestro spun the boy around and glowered at him suspiciously. His coarse, jowly face was nearly as red as the droplet of wine that was trickling down his chin. He grabbed the corner of the drawing between two fingers and flipped it over, hiding the diagram.

"What are you doing here, thief?" he demanded.

His breath gusted over Leonardo and the wine fumes almost made him swoon. He tried to wriggle loose, but Silvestro's thick fingers just tightened their grip on his shoulder.

"I am no thief," Leonardo protested. "I was sent here by Maestro Andrea del Verrocchio."

"A spy!" Silvestro exclaimed. "That pig has sent you here to steal my secrets and turn them to his own profit. Well, whatever you have seen, it will do you no good."

Silvestro's fingers dug into his shoulder with bruising force.

"I'm no spy either," Leonardo persisted desperately. "I am simply delivering a message." He groped for the sealed note and handed it to the artist as a peace offering.

Silvestro scowled at the letter without taking it. "What is it?" he demanded.

Leonardo squirmed, realising that a demand for money would only enrage Silvestro further.

"It did not befit my lowly station to inquire," he said, laying the paper down gingerly on the edge of the table. "But I am sure it is a message redolent of the deep respect Maestro Andrea has expressed for you on many occasions. Do not trouble yourself to open it until you have the leisure to enjoy its eloquent contents to the full. Perhaps tonight after supper..."

Silvestro's grip loosened slightly. Leonardo wriggled free and backed out of the door. He retreated across the workshop, bowing as he went, only too well aware of the apprentices sniggering at him. When he saw Silvestro take a step towards him, Leonardo swung round and raced out into the street.

He beat a hasty retreat from the unsavoury neighbourhood of the Oltrarno and did not slow his pace until he was safely across the Ponte Vecchio. On the north side of the Arno, he paused for breath, leaning on a wall and gazing down into the water.

The sight brought back the memory of a day last year when Leonardo had perched on a rocky ledge hanging out over the same river many miles to the north. He had longed then to spread his arms out like wings and fly off like a bird, leaving behind the dull routine of the family farm.

Distracted by his daydream, he had lost his footing and plunged headlong into the river. Flailing about in the water, he had managed to grab the trailing branch of a bent old tree and pull himself up. If not for that, Leonardo might have been sucked under by the current and drowned.

The memory was enough to set his heart pounding like a hammer. Turning abruptly away from the river, he hurried up the street into the heart of the city.

The Piazza della Signoria was filled with noise and bustle. All around the vast open square, merchants, entertainers, preachers and politicians were vying for the attention of the passers-by. A large crowd had gathered before the steps of the palace where the Signoria held their meetings. An excited figure was haranguing them, waving his clenched fist in the air as he spoke.

"This is what the Medici will bring down upon us, a war with Venice," he warned shrilly. "And for what? For the sake of an upstart who is the son of an upstart, a bandit who has stolen the title of Duke of Milan."

The crowd booed the name of Medici and yelled in agreement with the orator. One man dared to call out against the speaker only to be quickly silenced by his neighbours.

From the other side of the square Leonardo could hear another speaker loudly praising the Medici to the cheers of his audience. Here and there he saw people accost strangers and demand their opinion with sharp voices and upraised fists.

In the past he had heard many noisy arguments being waged in this square, but they were usually resolved with a jug of wine and good-natured laughter. Over the past few weeks, however, these lively debates had become charged with hostility and threats of violence.

It all reminded him of the angry exchange he had overheard at Silvestro's workshop. Then, as if conjured up out of that memory, he saw the man in the green cloak crossing the square directly ahead of him.

Leonardo pulled up short and ducked behind a trio of black-robed nuns whose way had been blocked by a wheedling pedlar. When the sisters moved off, Leonardo was relieved to see that the sinister stranger now had his back to him. He had fallen in with a gang of men led by a lanky fellow with bright red hair and a long, pointed nose.

Are they involved in the same plot as Silvestro? Leonardo wondered.

He edged nearer, trying to catch what they were saying. The distinctive rasp of the green-cloaked man stood out from the voices of the others, but Leonardo could not distinguish his words. Suddenly, the stranger made a chopping gesture with his hand and departed, heading off towards the north side of the square.

Leonardo hesitated only a moment. He would surely be expected back at the workshop by now, but for what? So he could spend the rest of the day spreading paste over canvas with a hogshair brush?

See and understand, Maestro Andrea had told him. And that was what he would do. He would follow this man, and in doing so, learn what it was Silvestro was so anxious to hide.

He started to tail the stranger, but he had only gone a few steps when the red-haired man stepped directly into his path. "Ho! Here's a fine young peacock! And yet he skulks about like a rat!"

Leonardo pulled up short and blinked at him. "I was proceeding about my business," he said, straightening his tunic. "By what right do you block my way?"

"The right every loyal citizen of Florence has to protect the public interest," the redhead answered. He leaned forward, his nose weaving from side to side as if he were trying to spear a fish. "Tell me, my young peacock, who you are for – the Hill or the Plain?"

The question was so ludicrous, Leonardo was actually annoyed. "If you want to argue about geography, go and bother someone else," he said curtly.

He immediately regretted his words, for the redhead's four friends now drew in around him. Some of them had cudgels stuck in their belts and they were fingering their weapons with an air of menace.

"I asked you a simple question," the red-haired man growled. "Are you for the Hill or the Plain?"

Leonardo had no notion what they wanted, but he was sure it would be a bad idea to give the wrong reply. He swallowed. "That's an important question."

"He is for the valley!" interposed a voice.

A burly young man with a thick, black beard elbowed his way into the circle. He was followed by a shorter fellow with a head of feathery golden curls that shone like a halo above his plump, cherubic face.

"What do you mean he is for the valley?" the red-haired man demanded. "What valley?"

The newcomer displayed a fist big enough to knock all of them flat with one blow. "The one between your ears," he replied, his broad chest swelling with laughter. He rapped his knuckles on top of the man's head and threw a brawny arm around Leonardo's shoulders.

"Come along," he said heartily, "I have better things for you to do than waste time with these idlers."

Leonardo beamed with relief. The golden-haired youth was his friend Sandro Botticelli and the other was Sandro's brother Simone. Together the three of them tried to move away, but the ruffians blocked their path.

One of them whipped out his cudgel and brandished it at Simone. Simone snatched the club from his hand and jabbed him in the stomach, knocking the wind out of him. Redhead and his friends uttered outraged curses, but none of them appeared eager to tackle the muscular Simone now he was armed.

Leonardo's eyes darted this way and that in expectation of an attack. He saw that more people were converging from every side, shouting challenges and threats.

"What's this? Pitti's thugs looking for trouble?"

"We'll put them in their place!"

"We'd like to see you try, you Medici lackeys!"

Supporters of the two sides began jostling and shoving each other, buffeting Leonardo and his friends from side to side like boats caught in a storm. Someone made a lunge for Simone only to be laid flat with one punch.

"We have to get out of here!" Sandro exclaimed as a rock flew past his head.

"Yes, but how?" asked Leonardo.

"Order! Order!" a voice barked over the hubbub. "Give way or be arrested!"

"Give way, I say!" bellowed another.

Both had foreign accents, German or Hungarian. Leonardo couldn't say which, but he could see a body of uniformed men driving a wedge between the rival factions.

"Praise Heaven!" gasped Sandro. "It's the city guard!"

The guardsmen were all foreign mercenaries under the command of a Constable who was also recruited from outside Florence. This was to ensure that the forces of law had no ties to any family or party in the city.

"Come on!" said Simone, seizing the other two by the arm and hauling them through the crowd.

Fortunately the mob was breaking up as the guardsmen pressed forward, seizing anyone who resisted. Once they were in the clear, Leonardo breathed a sigh of relief.

"You push things too far, Simone," said Sandro with a shake of the head. "It would have been enough to get Leonardo away from there without provoking them."

"Hah!" scoffed Simone. "We were in no danger from those lackwits."

The brothers were entirely unlike each other except in one respect. They had a similarly stocky build which had earned them the nickname Botticelli – the Little Barrels. In Simone's case it was mostly muscle.

Sandro was one of the young artists who assisted at Maestro Andrea's workshop. It was there that he and Leonardo had met and become friends. Leonardo had dined several times at the boisterous Botticelli household with Sandro, his parents, his three brothers and their wives.

"What was all that about hills and plains?" Leonardo asked.

"Pitti and his cronies are called the party of the Hill," Simone explained, "because he is building that monstrosity for himself on the high ground in the Oltrarno."

Leonardo nodded. "And what about the Plain?"

"That is the party of the Medici family," said Simone, "who built their great house on the flat ground on this side of the river. Everybody is supposed to support one side or the other. Ridiculous, isn't it?"

"Dangerous, I'd say," said Leonardo. "It's a lucky thing you came by."

"Yes, I was just fetching my brother here from the home of the wealthy Donati family," said Simone with a sly wink.

Leonardo saw then that Sandro was carrying a satchel filled with all his artist's equipment. "What were you doing there?" he asked.

"I have a commission," Sandro replied, beaming proudly. "I have been engaged to paint a portrait of Lucrezia Donati."

"The most beautiful woman in all of Florence!" Simone added, giving his brother a playful dig in the ribs.

"Lucrezia Donati!" Leonardo exclaimed. "I've heard whole tournaments have been held in her honour."

Sandro raised his blue eyes soulfully to Heaven as though he were seeing a vision. "She is an ideal of womanhood, Leonardo. Words cannot encompass such beauty, only the skill of a dedicated artist."

"But you?" said Leonardo incredulously. "You've only just left your master Fra Lippi's workshop! How did you land this prize?"

"Lucrezia is the sweetheart of Lorenzo de' Medici, the son of the most important man in Florence," Sandro explained. "Lorenzo is frequently sent off as an ambassador to faraway cities, and he wants a small portrait of Lucrezia to take with him wherever he goes. In particular he wants it completed before he leaves for Naples in a few days' time."

"Yes, but how did he come to pick you?" Leonardo pressed him.

Sandro frowned briefly at the interruption then carried on. "He was at Fra Lippi's workshop, inquiring if my former master might do this painting for him. Fra Lippi was much too busy to do it at short notice, but he recommended me. I was summoned to the Medici house to show Lorenzo some samples of my work, and he was impressed enough to engage my services."

Leonardo's mouth puckered. "I wish I could have a share of your good luck," he said gloomily. "I have nothing to look forward to but chores and practice."

"Your turn will come," Sandro said. "After all, you've scarcely started your apprenticeship."

"In the mean time," said Simone, "we have important business to attend to." He laid a hand on Leonardo's shoulder and began steering him away from the square.

"But my master—" Leonardo protested, pointing back in the direction of the Via dell'Agnolo.

"Can do without you for a little longer," Simone finished for him. "My friends and I are short-handed, and I need you and Sandro to save the day. Now hurry, because we're already late."

"Late for what?" Leonardo asked.

"A battle to the death!" Simone answered with a wicked grin.

4

The Lion of Anchiano

Leonardo was dragged out into the middle of the football field, protesting that he needed to change his clothes.

"No time," Simone told him. "The game's already started and those woolworkers have got us outnumbered. You have played before, haven't you?"

"I've kicked a ball around back home," said Leonardo, "but nothing like this."

The football green was squeezed into the western corner of the city walls, flanked on one side by an orchard and on the other by a slaughterhouse. Each team boasted nearly thirty men, the goldsmiths distinguished by their yellow sashes, the woolworkers in red. Many of them already bore cuts and bruises, and they were taunting each other with insults and obscene gestures.

"There's no use arguing," Sandro advised his friend. "When it comes to playing against the woolworkers, nothing matters to Simone except victory."

"And how do we win?" Leonardo asked uneasily.

"Get the ball over the enemy goal line," replied Sandro with a shrug. "That's as much as I can understand. I wouldn't be here at all, but family is family."

With a ragged cheer the goldsmiths gathered around the Botticelli brothers. "It's about time you got here, Simone. We're already one goal down."

"Don't worry, lads," said Simone, slapping Leonardo on the back. "I've brought along a secret weapon. This is Leonardo da Vinci, as quick and skilful a player as ever kicked a ball."

"He looks fit enough," somebody commented.

"But he's dressed for courting, not sporting," joked a wiry youth with a mop of curly black hair. There was a round of crude laughter.

"Don't let these pretty feathers fool you, Jacopo," said Simone. "He's a craftsman like us, a worker in stone, metal and wood, not a milksop scholar. Back in his home village they call him the Lion of Anchiano."

A wild whoop greeted the ball as it came arcing through the air from the other end of the field. Before it hit the ground, both teams charged in to the attack.

"What's this 'Lion of Anchiano' nonsense?" Leonardo asked as he caught up with Simone.

Simone grinned broadly. "I've given you a reputation. Now all you have to do is live up to it. Grab the ball and run with it if you can. Otherwise kick it upfield to one of our lads."

The teams collided with a roar and Leonardo was tossed about like a piece of driftwood. A mad flurry of kicking and gouging ensued. He was shoved, elbowed, kneed, punched and even spat on.

It seemed one of the unspoken aims of the game was to inflict as much injury on the opposing team as the loose rules allowed. Several times Leonardo was knocked to the ground and had to scramble to his feet to avoid being trampled. But he soon learned to give as good as he got, shouldering woolworkers aside in the fight to get his hands on the ball.

It was briefly his, until another goldsmith snatched it away and booted it upfield. With a bound, the agile Jacopo plucked it from the air and made for the goal line. Everyone stampeded after. Leonardo joined the race, yelling encouragement to his team-mate. Jacopo raced on, leaping over the line a good three strides ahead of his pursuers.

A resounding cheer went up from the goldsmiths. With the score now tied, both sides trooped back to midfield to begin again.

In that short breathing space, Leonardo discovered to his horror that his fine satin shirt and scarlet hose were hopelessly muddied and torn. Even as he contemplated the grass stains on his knees, a passing woolworker jostled his elbow.

"Not so fancy now, are you?"

Leonardo's temper flared and he stalked towards the centre of the field.

Sandro joined him as they awaited the kick off, his cherubic face bright red under his sweaty mop of golden curls. "Too many pastries," he panted ruefully.

Before Leonardo could comment, the woolworkers kicked the ball back into play. He dived in with a vengeance. One more goal would clinch it.

Out of the press of scuffling bodies the ball suddenly popped skyward. Curving through the air it dropped unexpectedly into Sandro's arms. The young artist froze in dismay. Howling and screeching, the woolworkers closed in on him from all sides like hungry wolves.

Upfield, Simone was waving frantically for the ball.

"Kick it away!" Leonardo yelled, racing to his friend's assistance.

Sandro remained paralysed, the grasping hands of the woolworkers almost upon him. With hardly a moment to spare, Leonardo snatched the ball from his friend. Spinning about, he booted it high upfield.

Simone jumped and caught it. In the next instant Leonardo and Sandro disappeared under an avalanche of bodies. Crushed beneath the weight, Leonardo fought for breath in the sweat-soaked darkness. Somewhere amid the grunts and curses he heard a pained yelp from Sandro.

Then a raucous bellow of triumph sounded across the field.

Simone had scored the winning goal.

One by one the players were dragged off the heaving pile, freeing the two victims at the bottom. Leonardo was hauled dizzily to his feet, flushed and gasping. The goldsmiths flocked around him, shaking his hand and clapping him on the back. The unexpected pleasure of finding himself a hero banished – for the time being – all thoughts of his ruined clothes.

"Come on, Sandro, we've won!"

But Sandro was still curled up on the ground, clutching his right wrist. He groaned. "No, no, no, I've lost. I've lost everything!"

Back at the Botticelli house Sandro's mother wound the bandage tightly around his injured wrist, tutting and muttering to herself all the while. He flinched as she gave it a final tug before standing back to regard her handiwork. Wrapped inside the bandage was a poultice of stewed nettles and vinegar that gave off a pungent odour.

"Now you keep that arm rested," the old woman instructed. "I'm going to the kitchen to mix you a broth of leeks and pig's trotters. That will put the colour back in your cheeks."

Sandro stared mutely at the green-stained bandage and wrinkled his nose.

"I'm sure it will be a help," Leonardo said politely, adding to himself, *if he survives drinking it.*

The old lady scuttled off, leaving the two young men alone for the first time since the end of the football game. Having completed his apprenticeship with Fra Filippo Lippi, Sandro had only recently set up as an artist in his own right. Until he could afford to open his own workshop, his father had allowed him to turn one of the storerooms at the back of the house into a temporary studio.

That was where they sat now, surrounded by sketches of saints, centaurs, Madonnas, satyrs and angels that were spread all over the walls.

"It's a rotten bit of luck, your arm getting stepped on like that," Leonardo said sympathetically.

Sandro raised his blue eyes slowly, as if unwilling to look upon a world that could be so cruel. "Who knows how long it will be before I can use a paintbrush again?" he moaned. "I took my first step on the ladder of success and the rung has snapped beneath my foot."

Leonardo felt a pang inside. Seeing the normally jolly Sandro brought low like this was like seeing the sun blotted out by an eclipse. "Can't Lorenzo just wait a bit longer for his portrait?" he suggested.

"I told you, he wants it before he leaves for Naples next week," said Sandro, "and wealthy families like the Medici are accustomed to getting what they want."

Leonardo nodded slowly, understanding the problem. He knew from his own father that it did not pay to inconvenience rich and powerful people. "There will be other clients, Sandro."

"Do you think so? For an artist who has broken his very first contract? No, this is ruin for me. I should have stayed behind in the Piazza della Signoria and taken my chances with Pitti's ruffians."

The mention of the confrontation in the square suddenly jogged Leonardo's memory. Something had been nagging at the back of his mind but events had been moving too fast for him to give it any thought.

"Sandro, didn't Simone say the Medici supporters called themselves the party of the Plain?"

"Plain, lake, mountain – what difference does it make?" Sandro sighed.

We shall bring destruction down on the plain, Silvestro had said. And Leonardo was sure it had something to do with the machine he was building.

He closed his eyes and visualised the scene in Silvestro's studio. As far back as he could remember, Leonardo had had a gift for recalling exactly any image he had seen. Now he placed himself back in that room, walked over to the desk. There was the diagram before him, each detail precise in itself, but its purpose still elusive. In order to study it properly, he would have to make a copy of his own.

Rising from his stool, he sidled towards a stack of drawing paper and fingered the topmost sheet. "Sandro, could I borrow some of this paper?"

"Help yourself," groaned Sandro, rubbing his injured wrist.

Leonardo took the sheet and laid it flat on a table by the window. Grabbing a stick of charcoal from a nearby pot, he quickly began sketching. A cog here, a wheel there, a cord, a weight. Yes, that looked right. As the machine took shape on the page, so a plan began to form in his mind.

When an opportunity comes your way, grab it with both hands before somebody steals it, his father had told him more than once.

"Sandro, you know that ladder of success you were talking about? Instead of climbing up rung by rung, how would you like to fly straight to the top?"

Sandro looked up with doleful eyes. "What do you mean?"

Leonardo picked up the paper and held it in front of Sandro.

"Look, I've made this copy of a diagram I saw at Maestro Silvestro's today. He's involved in some sort of plot against the Medici – I'm sure of it."

Leonardo repeated all he had overheard and described how he had seen the stranger again in the Piazza della Signoria.

Sandro squinted at the drawing. "But this is just a lot of sticks ands wheels," he protested. "It's no threat to anybody."

"Look, Sandro, suppose the Medici are in some sort of danger. Wouldn't they be more than grateful to anyone who could warn them of that? Wouldn't they reward them with a lifetime of well paid work? There would be no more broken ladders for you."

And no more drudgery in the workshop for me, he thought. He could trade the gratitude of the Medici for a commission of his own!

"And why would they listen to either of us?" Sandro objected. "You are a mere apprentice and I'll be lucky if they don't throw me in jail for breach of contract."

"You give in too easily, Sandro," Leonardo scolded him. "The contract isn't broken yet. There must be something you can do."

Sandro pondered for a moment then brightened. "You're right, Leonardo," he said, jumping to his feet. "I will go to church at once, to the Chapel of the Innocents. I will pray for Lorenzo to come down with a fever until I have recovered. But no." He struck himself on the brow with the flat of his hand. "What manner of Christian am I to wish such a thing on my patron! No, a brief falling out between him and Lucrezia, that would be enough."

Leonardo folded up the drawing and tucked it away inside his tunic. "Sandro, you're being totally impractical –

as usual. All you really need is someone to help you finish the portrait."

"You make it sound so easy," Sandro sighed. "What artist worthy of the name would let his work pass under the name of another?"

Leonardo laid a hand on his friend's shoulder. "An artist wouldn't, but an apprentice might." He added pointedly, "A very *talented* apprentice."

5

A Bird in Flight

When Leonardo came out of the workshop the next day, he walked straight into an ambush. He had scarcely gone a dozen yards down the Via dell'Agnolo when he was seized and hauled into the dingy alley beside the coppersmith's shop.

Before he could cry out, a grimy palm clamped itself over his mouth. His arms were pinned to his sides from behind and a glint of metal appeared under his left eye.

It was a chisel that had been honed to a razor-sharp edge.

"If you know what's good for you, you'll keep quiet," hissed a voice.

Leonardo recognised the speaker: Silvestro's apprentice, Pimple-face, breathing fish fumes and garlic into his face. Twitcher must be behind him, holding his arms.

Pimple-face slipped his hand from Leonardo's mouth but kept the chisel close enough to slice his cheek open if he tried to call for help. With his free hand he felt inside the leather satchel strapped to Leonardo's belt.

"What's he got there?" Twitcher asked.

"The usual stuff – brushes, palette knife, paint rags," Pimple-face replied. He looked Leonardo over. "Not dressed so handsome today, are you, *Leonardo da Vinci*?"

"Somebody steal your fancy gear?" taunted Twitcher.

Leonardo was wearing the drab working clothes he had come to Florence in while his one good outfit was being washed and repaired after yesterday's misadventure. Determined to protect his dignity, he responded stiffly, "I only dress up for special occasions."

"Like visiting old Silvestro, you mean?" sneered the Twitcher.

"That's what we come about," said Pimple-face. "When you was visiting, you didn't see nothing, right?"

Leonardo squirmed. "I don't know what you mean. I only came to deliver a message."

"Oh yes, the bill," chortled Twitcher. "Old Silvestro was fit to throttle his own grandma when he opened it."

"And he was even madder when we told him we saw you nosing around," said Pimple-face. "He sent word to his client."

"Now this client, he don't like nosy people," said Twitcher. "He told Silvestro to *take care of it*."

Pimple-face leered unpleasantly. "So here we are." He grabbed the front of Leonardo's tunic and pressed the chisel against his cheek.

Leonardo swallowed hard. His copy of Silvestro's diagram was tucked inside the tunic, perilously close to Pimple-face's clutching fist. He had spent half the night finishing the drawing, borrowing one of Gabriello's candles so he'd have enough light to work by.

"An artist's work is his own private business," said Pimple-face. "Understand?"

Leonardo couldn't nod without cutting his face. "I understand," he breathed.

"What did you see?"

Leonardo could feel his heart pounding against the folded drawing. "Nothing," he replied meekly.

Pimple-face released his grip and patted Leonardo on the head like a clever dog. "That's right, you didn't see nothing, you don't know nothing, and you don't remember nothing."

With the edge of the chisel still so close to his face, Leonardo wished for a moment that were true.

At a gesture from Pimple-face, Twitcher released him. Sniggering, the two apprentices scuttled off into the crowd that was passing along the Via dell'Agnolo.

Leonardo slumped against the wall and felt his cheek to make sure the skin wasn't broken. Things were getting more dangerous than he had anticipated. Was it worth risking his life just to gain favour with the Medici? No, only a fool would get caught in the middle of this power struggle.

He pressed a hand to where the drawing was hidden. Maybe he should burn it before Silvestro and his friends discovered he had made a copy of their design. But no, he could not help feeling that this was the key to his future, his chance to enter a wider world.

The clang of a nearby church bell made Leonardo start. He would have to sort this out later. He was already late. He darted out of the alley and ran the rest of the way to the market.

Sandro was at the agreed meeting place: beside the statue of Abundance in the centre of Florence's Old Market.

"Where have you been?" he exclaimed when he spotted Leonardo emerging from the crowd. "I've been waiting for ages."

Raising his voice above the hubbub of barter, Leonardo said, "I couldn't leave until I finished all the chores Maestro Andrea had for me." He had decided to say nothing about his encounter with Silvestro's apprentices until he was certain of what to do.

They were surrounded by butchers' stalls and the air was buzzing with insects drawn to the raw meat. Sandro swatted away a fly with his uninjured hand. "Well, it hasn't done my stomach any good, I can tell you. Every time I think of this plan of yours, it hurts like there was a sea urchin rolling around inside it."

He set off, awkwardly manoeuvring his way around a pair of squabbling vendors. Leonardo wove through the crowd, keeping in step with his friend.

"There is one thing we need to settle first," Leonardo said, drawing level. "My fee."

Sandro stopped by a fish stall where trout, pike and eels lay on the slab. The eyes of the fish were wide and their mouths agape, as if they were still surprised at being netted.

Sandro gave Leonardo an equally startled look. "Your fee?"

"Why are you so shocked? Don't tell me you're doing this portrait for free."

"That's different. I'm an artist and you're only an apprentice."

"Apprentice or not, this is professional work I'm doing," Leonardo said in his most reasonable voice. "Maestro Andrea says that money is the lifeblood of art."

"Friends should not discuss such matters," said Sandro, walking on. "*Money is the poison that blights the flower of affection.*"

"What's that supposed to be – a proverb?"

Sandro shrugged. "It's what my brothers always say when I try to borrow money from them."

They were passing a trader whose caged birds were stacked one on top of the other like bricks in a wall. At the top of the stack was a lark that was beating its wings feverishly against the bars of its cage. Being so close to the sky seemed to make its confinement even more unbearable.

Leonardo knew how it felt. "I'll tell you what," he

suggested, "why don't you give me a gift of some sort?"

"I suppose that would be acceptable," Sandro conceded, "as long as it's a very small gift."

"All right – that bird," Leonardo said, pointing.

Sandro tilted his head and gave the bird a dubious look. "It doesn't look very clean."

"Look, just buy me the bird and we'll call that my fee."

"Six soldi," said the birdseller, holding out his hand.

"That's outrageous!" objected Sandro.

"Do you want to spend the rest of the day arguing," demanded Leonardo, "or do you want to get to the Torre Donati while there is still light to paint by?"

Sandro sighed and reached into his money pouch. Carefully, he counted the coins into the birdseller's hand. "I hope you appreciate that you have made me destitute."

"Don't worry," said Leonardo, lifting down the cage. "Soon you will be famous and wealthy enough to buy a thousand birds."

He inspected the latch on the cage. It was a simple loop of wire and he easily worked it loose. The cage swung open and the bird hopped out on to his outstretched palm.

"What are you doing?" asked Sandro, aghast. "It's going to—"

The lark took flight. Whipping the folded paper out of

his tunic, Leonardo used the back of it to make some rapid sketches of the bird as it soared off. It left the market behind, arcing gracefully across the sky to disappear behind the dome of the Duomo, Florence's cathedral.

"That's my money flying away!" Sandro exclaimed.

Leonardo surveyed his work. "What's the point in having a bird if you can't watch it fly?"

Sandro peered over his friend's shoulder. In mere moments Leonardo had made several lightning sketches of the bird in flight, showing in sequence the movements of its wings and tail as it soared over the rooftops.

"How could you see all that?" Sandro asked. "It was too quick."

"Not if you pay attention," said Leonardo. He tapped himself on the temple with his stick of charcoal. "Everything I see is stored up here like a stack of pictures one on top of the other."

"Well, you don't need to go to all that trouble just to paint a bird," said Sandro.

"It's not about painting," Leonardo explained. "I want to understand how it flies."

"It flies because that's what it's meant to do," said Sandro. "A bird is meant to fly in the air, a fish is meant to swim in the sea, a man is meant to walk on the ground."

"And an apprentice is meant to keep to his place," Leonardo added under his breath. "Well, we'll see about that."

They soon arrived at the Torre Donati, a lofty fortress of yellow stone. Sandro gripped the brass knocker, which was in the shape of a dragon's head, and rapped three times on the door. It was opened by a plump, fastidious man in a crimson tunic who waved them brusquely inside.

"Tomasso, the chamberlain," Sandro whispered to Leonardo. "This is my assistant, Leonardo da Vinci," he informed the chamberlain. "Is your mistress ready for the sitting?"

Tomasso took a backward step and called out, "Fresina!"

A girl of about thirteen came scampering from a room at the back of the house. She had a slender face and long yellow hair tied in plaits. She also wore the distinctive grey robe of a slave.

"Fresina, go to your mistress," Tomasso instructed. "Tell her the painter is here."

He emphasised the word 'painter' as though he were announcing that the weekly delivery of garden manure had arrived.

The girl bobbed her head and scurried off.

"I believe you know the way," Tomasso said to Sandro.

"You'd think he was the master of the house," said Leonardo, as Sandro led the way up a flight of steps.

"We artists are an insignificant group compared to the bankers, merchants and clothmakers who run the city," said Sandro. "Our job is simply to serve the needs of the rich, the same way a cook or a tailor does."

They entered a spacious room on the topmost floor where the sun slanted through the westward facing window. The chamber itself was panelled in polished oak. On one wall hung a tapestry depicting the Labours of Hercules while under the window stood a large chest decorated with pictures of a deer hunt.

Near the centre of the room stood an easel on which there was a small picture about one foot square. Leonardo walked over and examined it. The chestnut hair, coiled in the latest fashion, was almost finished, as were the delicate ears. The eyebrows had been sketched in, and there were the faintest lines of a nose, but the rest of the face was blank.

"It's quite good, as far as it's done," Leonardo said.

"Whatever you do, don't spoil it," said Sandro anxiously. "Make sure you follow my style. Never forget that the way to please your subjects is to bring them to perfection in the portrait. Imagine they have been carried up to Heaven and paint them as they would appear there."

"I don't know what people look like in Heaven," said Leonardo. "I can only paint what I see."

Sandro began unpacking his art supplies and setting them out on the table to the left of the easel. "You will have to mix the paints on the palette," he said. "My wrist is plaguing me like a wound today."

"Leave it to me," said Leonardo.

He set to work preparing the various hues and colours he would need to complete the portrait. Sandro pestered him throughout the whole process, giving him unwanted advice about the use of white lead and viridian green.

Leonardo lifted up the palette. "If you don't stop fussing like a fretful mother, I'll crack this over your skull," he warned.

It was at that moment that Lucrezia Donati walked into the room.

6

The Girl in the Tower

Leonardo's heart missed a beat. He wondered at once if any portrait could do justice to those dark, almond-shaped eyes, which grew wide at the sight of the raised palette. In the next instant they crinkled with mirth as Lucrezia laughed.

"What is going on? Has a war broken out?" she inquired. "Is there not enough uproar in the streets without our artists turning on each other?"

Lucrezia's mouth was as animated as her eyes, changing shape rapidly with every syllable she spoke. A thousand different expressions could be glimpsed beneath the surface of that beautiful face.

Leonardo managed to tear his gaze away from her. He tilted the palette towards the window and squinted. "I was just holding it up to observe how the colours catch the light," he said.

"Yes, it's very important how the colours catch the light," said Sandro, placing a finger on the edge of the palette and pushing it gently down towards the table.

The slave girl Fresina entered behind her mistress, carrying wine and sweetmeats on a tray. She placed it on a small side table by the door and Lucrezia dismissed her with a wave.

"She has very unusual colouring," Sandro noted, following the slave girl with his gaze as she left.

"How like an artist! Couldn't you just say you find her very pretty?" Lucrezia mocked him gently.

Sandro's face reddened and he cleared his throat nervously. "Where does she come from?"

"From Circassia, on the far shore of the Black Sea," Lucrezia replied. "Father purchased her at the market in Venice. He says Circassian slaves are better behaved than Tartars and work harder than Russians. And their women are renowned for their beauty."

There was only one thought on Leonardo's mind and he couldn't help blurting it out. "The only beauty that concerns us today is that which stands before us."

Lucrezia's long eyelashes fluttered in amusement. "That was very gallant," she observed, "and you actually sounded as if you meant it. Is there a knight out of the old romances hidden beneath that humble garb?"

Leonardo felt a flush come to his cheek and hoped Lucrezia was not aware of it. He removed his cap with a flourish and bowed. "Leonardo da Vinci."

"And what brings you here today, Leonardo?"

"He is a pupil of my good friend, the artist Andrea del Verrocchio," Sandro interposed. "Andrea has asked me to help him develop his technique."

"In what way?"

"Maestro Sandro Botticelli has kindly agreed to allow me to make a small contribution to his portrait of you," said Leonardo.

"A *very* small contribution," Sandro emphasised. "A few background details, no more than that, but enough to improve his handling of draperies and woodwork."

"Is that what he's going to do now?" asked Lucrezia.

"Why, yes," said Sandro. "We were just preparing the paints when you came in."

"In that case, you won't need me." She turned to the door.

"Oh, but we do!" Leonardo exclaimed. "A portrait must be whole, the subject reflected in the background and all the surrounding objects."

"Exactly," Sandro agreed. "Never underestimate the importance of harmonising the shades of the room with the lovely colouring of the subject." He steered Lucrezia towards the small seat by the wall and sat her down.

"Now if you would just resume the pose of yesterday." With a gentle finger he tilted her head away from the canvas.

Leonardo was relieved: it was vital that she not be aware he was actually painting her face. Quickly, he finished mixing the colours and set about completing the line of her nose which Sandro had left unfinished. Sandro was doing his best to distract her with amusing talk.

The work was more challenging and more wonderful than Leonardo could have imagined. He had made copies of paintings as part of his training, and he had painted original landscapes of his own. But even in repose there was such energy in Lucrezia's features that painting her was like trying to capture the hundred different moods of the sea or the flight of a lark across the sky.

By the time he reached her chin, Lucrezia was growing impatient. "This is taking a long time for a few insignificant background details," she said.

"Alas, he is a slow worker," said Sandro dolefully. "The left hand, you see. No, do not look! It is important that you keep your head absolutely still."

Lucrezia sighed deeply and maintained her pose.

"I will check his progress," said Sandro.

He came to Leonardo's side and frowned at the portrait. "This here," he said in a low voice, "it's too dark." He was pointing at the lips.

"This is exactly as I see it," said Leonardo tightly.

"It's not right," Sandro insisted. "Here, let me show you."

Forgetting his injured arm, he made a grab for the brush. Leonardo fended him off and there was a brief struggle, ending with a cry of pain from Sandro. He jerked back, his teeth clenched in agony, but he did not move fast enough to hide the bandage on his wrist.

Lucrezia jumped up and ran to him. "What is the matter? Have you hurt yourself?"

She gently took his forearm and eased it away from his body. Sandro was helpless to resist.

"It's nothing. He's fine," said Leonardo, trying to steer her back to her seat.

But it was too late. Lucrezia was already staring at the portrait, at her face which was nearly complete. "You haven't been painting the background at all!"

She looked from the portrait, to Leonardo, to Sandro's injured wrist cradled in her hands. "I see you are unable to paint, Signor Botticelli, but why go to such lengths?"

Sandro hung his head. "The deception was not for your sake, but because of Lorenzo de' Medici," he confessed. "I did not want him to discover that I could not complete my commission. This is my first work for anyone of importance and if I fail to deliver it on time, I shudder to think of the consequences."

Lucrezia was only half listening. She was absorbed in the painting. She lifted a finger to adjust her hair, looking as though she expected the portrait to do the same. "I can scarcely believe this was painted by a stranger," she said. "Even in this unfinished state I see so much of myself here, I believe my portrait and I could swap places and no one would know the difference."

She turned to Leonardo and he could feel her gazing at him with the same intensity as she had examined the portrait. It was as if the painting had opened a door between them and she could now see him with the same clarity with which he had painted her.

"It is a great gift you have, to see so much," said Lucrezia.

Leonardo found himself nervously fingering the hem of his tunic. "I… I am glad you are pleased," he stammered.

"He has potential," Sandro conceded. "Of course, I had already made a start and given him detailed instructions on how to continue."

At the sound of Sandro's voice Lucrezia turned to him and the spell was broken. Leonardo felt as if the light in the room had Suddenly dimmed.

"But how did you think to keep up the pretence?" Lucrezia asked. "I was bound to see the picture before you left."

"Sandro was going to pretend to be painting the very part which I had already done," Leonardo explained. "In fact, his brush would not touch the canvas. I would keep you sufficiently distracted so you would not notice."

Impish amusement played about Lucrezia's lips. "Very resourceful," she complimented them.

"But now, of course, it is all for nothing." Sandro sighed.

Lucrezia's smile grew wider and her eyes flashed mischievously. "Only if I tell Lorenzo."

"You mean you will keep my secret?"

"It's such an ingenious trick," said Lucrezia, "I would not want to spoil it any more than I would want to spoil the painting itself. Besides, Lorenzo thinks himself so very clever. This would pay him back prettily for the trick he played on my cousin last week. Poor Giuseppi! Lorenzo and his friends carried his bed from his house while he was sleeping, so that he woke up in the middle of the Piazza Santa Trinita."

Sandro fell to his knees and kissed the girl's hand. "You have the kindness of a saint!"

"I don't know about that," Lucrezia giggled. "But I do hope a sense of fun wouldn't be out of place in Heaven."

Leonardo laughed too, but their sense of relief was interrupted by an urgent rap at the door.

"Come!" said Lucrezia.

The slender face of Fresina appeared. "Mistress," she said, "Signor Lorenzo de' Medici is on his way up. He says he wants to view the portrait."

"Thank you, Fresina," said Lucrezia. She waved the girl away and slammed the door shut.

Sandro grabbed Leonardo by the shoulder and propelled him towards the window.

"Quick!" he ordered. "Get in the chest!"

7

A Well-built Prison

Sandro flipped open the catch and threw up the lid. "Come on, get in!" he said, pointing to the empty interior of the chest.

"Are you crazy?" Leonardo exclaimed. "I'm not getting in there!"

"But you have to," Sandro insisted, his eyes feverish with panic. "If Lorenzo finds you here, he'll know exactly what's going on."

"He's right," Lucrezia agreed. "Lorenzo will see the paint is fresh and wonder why Signor Botticelli has stopped. He will spot the bandage, and even worse, he will see that your hands, Leonardo, are covered with paint."

Leonardo spread out his hands and stared at them in horror. Paint had smeared over his fingers during his brief struggle with Sandro and it was as incriminating as blood.

"But there isn't enough room," he protested.

"Yes, there is," said Sandro. "Have you learned nothing from studying perspective?"

With Sandro prodding him on, Leonardo clambered reluctantly into the chest. Lucrezia pressed his artist's satchel into Leonardo's arms before Sandro pushed him down on to his knees.

"This would be easier if you were a bit shorter," Sandro grunted. "Bow your shoulders and tuck in your chin. And be quiet!"

With those final words he slammed the lid shut.

From inside the darkness of his prison, Leonardo heard the door of the room open. Then a curiously high-pitched, nasal voice spoke.

"Lucrezia, Signor Botticelli – hard at work I see."

"Lorenzo, I was not expecting you," said Lucrezia lightly.

"I hope that doesn't make me any less welcome," Lorenzo countered playfully.

"Not at all," Lucrezia laughed. "I was getting tired of

posing and your arrival gives me the excuse to persuade Signor Botticelli to abandon his work for the day."

She sounded completely casual and relaxed, not at all as if she had someone shut up inside a linen chest.

"When I heard you were here, Signor Botticelli, I was happy for the chance to witness your skilful hand at work," said Lorenzo.

Inside the chest Leonardo winced at the choice of words. The last thing they wanted was for Lorenzo to spot Sandro's injury.

Sandro cleared his throat nervously. "Of course, I would be happy to continue, but if the lady is wearying..."

"And the sun is almost gone," Lucrezia added. "It is not possible to continue."

"Well, while there is enough light left to see by, let me have a look at the work in progress," said Lorenzo.

"Would it not be better to wait until it is finished?" Sandro suggested. Leonardo could hear the note of alarm in his voice.

"Pah!" Lorenzo exclaimed good-humouredly. "Even a half-finished image of Lucrezia will delight the eye twice as much as a finished portrait of any other woman in Florence."

Leonardo heard footsteps making their way to the easel.

He could hear his own heart beating faster in the darkness. He didn't know whether it was because he feared Lorenzo would uncover their deception or because he was awaiting his verdict on the painting.

What manner of man is this Lorenzo de' Medici? he wondered again. The heir of the most powerful man in Florence, the sweetheart of the beautiful Lucrezia. Surely he must be a handsome and regal individual in spite of his curious voice.

Leonardo decided he had to see for himself. He put a hand to the lid and eased it open a fraction, a gap no more than the width of a finger. There, standing by the painting, was Lorenzo, and Leonardo could not have been more amazed.

What he saw was a young man of average height who looked to be no more than sixteen years old. Far from looking like a handsome noble, he was as plain as a peasant, with a bulbous nose indented at the bridge and a chin that jutted out like the buttress of a cathedral. His straight black hair hung down to his shoulders like a widow's shawl.

Even Sandro, who was always so eager to please, would have a hard time making a handsome portrait out of that face, Leonardo thought.

Lorenzo folded his arms and regarded the painting. "Already I can see the beauty of her features emerging from the canvas," he said, "like the figurehead of a ship emerging from the fog. It will be completed by the week's end?"

"Certainly," Sandro replied. Even in that one word Leonardo could hear Sandro's relief that his patron had not spotted anything suspicious. But then Sandro caught sight of the tell-tale chink below the lid of the chest and bit his lip in alarm.

"My father expects me to leave for Naples any day now," said Lorenzo, "and I must have this picture with me."

He turned away from the portrait towards the window, as if he could glimpse that far-off city already. Sandro quickly stepped in front of him, blocking Lorenzo's view of the chest. "Ah, yes, your embassy to Naples," he said. "Embassies, alliances, you cannot have too many of them."

Lorenzo laughed. "Tell that to Luca Pitti and his cronies."

"Perhaps we should leave and let Signor Botticelli pack up his things," Lucrezia interposed with a twinkle. "I'm sure he wants to get home to his supper."

"Now that brings me to why I came here in the first

place," Lorenzo declared enthusiastically. "I am on my way to the home of Leon Battista Alberti."

"Alberti the artist?" asked Sandro. He inched his way backwards, closer and closer to the chest until he had completely blocked Leonardo's view.

"Yes," Lorenzo continued, "and also Alberti the architect, the athlete, the writer, the historian, the engineer. Not only is he the most brilliant conversationalist in the whole of Tuscany, he lays a table that would convert a hermit to gluttony. I knew, Lucrezia, that you would want to come with me."

"Sometimes, Lorenzo, you know my mind so well, it makes me wish I had some secrets to keep from you," Lucrezia laughed.

"And you shall come too, Signor Botticelli," Lorenzo added.

"Er, I have several things..." Sandro mumbled. He sat down heavily on the chest, forcing the lid shut and plunging Leonardo into darkness once more.

"Nothing that can't wait, I'm sure," said Lorenzo. "No, you must come. I insist upon it!"

There was an element of steel in Lorenzo's tone, and yet he had lost none of his pleasant charm. For the first time Leonardo could believe that this was indeed someone who was learning to wield power. But he still seemed a poor match for Lucrezia's beauty and wit.

"I think it would be wise to accept Lorenzo's invitation," Lucrezia said pointedly. "Think of all the potential patrons you could meet."

"Yes, of course, patrons," said Sandro blankly.

"Come, I have a carriage outside with plenty of room for all of us," Lorenzo said jovially.

Sandro was pulled to his feet and Leonardo could hear him being ushered out of the door with lavish descriptions of the feast that awaited them. Once their voices had passed beyond his hearing, he waited a few minutes to make sure everyone had left the building.

Deciding at last that it was safe to emerge from hiding, he pressed one hand against the lid and gave a shove. It didn't budge.

Aghast, Leonardo pushed again, harder. Still the lid wouldn't shift. When Sandro sat down on the chest he must have jolted the clasp down into the locked position.

Leonardo was trapped!

His first impulse was to cry out for help, but not only could he not face the humiliation of being found like this, he could not risk exposing the deception they had played on Lorenzo de' Medici.

The only way to save the situation was to get himself out of the box and then slip out of the house unnoticed. All that was holding him in was a metal clasp hooked on to a small peg sticking out of the side of the chest. Surely that was not so much to overcome.

He arched his back and pushed up against the lid, trying to break the clasp. Strain as he might, he soon realised that he did not have enough space to exert any leverage. He rocked this way and that, thumping and kicking at the chest's interior. He tried to detect some sign that the wood was buckling at the seams, but nothing moved.

Puffing from the effort, he cursed the skill of the Florentine craftsman who had constructed so stout a prison. He realised he might have no other recourse than to shriek for assistance, whatever the consequences.

With a groan of frustration he slumped against the side of the chest. His artist's satchel dug him in the ribs. Only then did he remember the contents of the bag: oil cloths, brushes, a stylus – and a palette knife.

After much awkward wriggling he managed to slide his hand into the bag. He groped blindly for the knife and felt his fingers close around the handle. He slipped it out and twisted into position.

Hoping the short blade would bear the strain, Leonardo

probed for the crack where the lid and the chest met. Pushing hard, he forced the tip of the blade into the hairline gap, then slid it along, seeking the clasp.

Metal met metal with a dull *chink*. Holding his breath, Leonardo painstakingly jiggled the knife handle up and down, forcing the blade forward. For an awful moment the clasp resisted.

Then it popped loose. Stifling a whoop of triumph, Leonardo raised the lid and stuck his head out. His first breath of fresh air was like a swallow of wine. He wiped a trembling hand across his sweaty brow and leaned over the side of the chest. All that remained now was to find a way to leave without being detected.

"Here! In here!"

The voice came from the passage on the other side of the door. There was the sound of a scuffle and the doorhandle began to turn. As the door swung open, Leonardo recoiled into the chest and hastily lowered the lid. He caught a fleeting glimpse of four figures before darkness swallowed him yet again.

He groaned inwardly. Was he ever going to get out of here?

"There is no other way," rasped a ruthless voice. "We must kill her now. It will take only a small cut."

"No!" protested another. "You cannot commit bloodshed here in my master's house."

"Your master?" a third man repeated sarcastically. "I am the one who holds your debts. I am your master – for all the use you have been to me."

There came a muffled noise, like someone trying to cry out.

"Hold her tightly!" snapped the third man. "She already got away from you once."

Stiffening, Leonardo realised that he recognised two of those voices. The first, harsh and foreign-sounding, he had heard arguing with Maestro Silvestro. The second was that of Tomasso, the chamberlain of the household. The third voice he did not know, but its tone was that of a man used to giving orders.

"She has heard too much," snapped the rasping voice. "Let us finish her and be gone."

"Keep that dagger back, Rodrigo!" the third man commanded. "We must be more subtle."

"That cushion there on the chair," suggested the rough-voiced Rodrigo. "Smother her and no one will know how she died. Who will care what happened to a slave?"

Leonardo's mouth had gone completely dry. In spite of the danger, he had to see what was going on. Setting the tips of his fingers against the lid, he eased it up the merest fraction.

Through the sliver of light he saw the chamberlain's crimson tunic, and the grey woollen robe of the slave girl Fresina. Shifting his head and squinting upward, he saw that Tomasso had the girl's arms fastened to her sides, one hand clamped over her mouth to keep her from crying out. Off to the left he could make out the glint of a dagger in a leather-gloved fist.

"Do it then, Tomasso!" the third voice ordered. "It is because of your carelessness we are in this situation."

The chamberlain quailed. "No, no! Spying for you is one thing, but I will not become a murderer."

There was a tense pause. "Very well," said the third voice. "Give the girl to me."

A richly dressed figure with a long, aristocratic face stepped into view and took charge of Fresina, carefully keeping her mouth covered. "If you haven't the stomach for it, then go," he told Tomasso. "And be sure to hold your tongue."

The chamberlain looked pathetically grateful as he backed towards the door. The next instant there came a sudden flash of steel and a dull thunk. Tomasso gave a strangled grunt and collapsed on the floor, Rodrigo's dagger protruding from his heart.

8

The Honour of Thieves

The horror of it took Leonardo's breath away. Through the narrow chink he stared at the body on the floor, scarcely able to believe his eyes. Rodrigo's hooded form glided forward and knelt to retrieve his bloody weapon.

"I did not tell you to kill him," said the aristocratic man irritably. He tightened his hold on Fresina who was struggling to break free.

"He would have talked," said Rodrigo. "Your hold on him was not strong enough to ensure his silence."

"But now we have a bloody corpse on our hands and we still have this girl to dispose of."

"There will be corpses enough before long," said Rodrigo. "What do two more matter?"

"Our plans are not yet ripe," said the other man, "and we cannot risk exposure now. We must think creatively." There was a moment of silence then he said, "Tear a piece of cloth from the girl's sleeve."

There came a ripping sound.

"Place it in the dead man's hand and fold his fingers over it," the leader directed. "Now smear some of the blood from your dagger over her clothes."

"I see," said Rodrigo approvingly. "It will look as if he caught her stealing and she stabbed him."

Fresina recoiled as Rodrigo approached her with the dagger, her blue eyes blazing with panic.

"Do not struggle, girl," he advised. "It will do you no good." Once the grisly work was done, he stepped back like an artist admiring the results of his labours.

"Now what do we do with our little murderess?" the leader wondered.

"Let me break her neck and fling her out of the window," said Rodrigo harshly. "It will appear she fell to her death attempting to escape from the house."

Leonardo's throat tightened. He had been a helpless witness to Tomasso's sudden death and now they were going to murder this innocent girl before his eyes. He couldn't just crouch here in hiding and let it happen, but what could he do against two armed men?

"Check the window and make sure the drop is sheer," the leader ordered.

The chest lay directly under the window. Leonardo shrank down as the hooded assassin approached, praying that he would not notice the opening under the lid. Rodrigo leaned over the chest, his legs blocking out the light.

Leonardo knew this was his only chance to save the girl, whatever the risk. Licking his dry lips, he tensed his limbs under him. With a wild cry, he jumped up.

The lid flew up and cracked Rodrigo on the jaw. He reeled backwards, stunned by the unexpected blow. Tumbling across the floor he crashed into a side table and brought the tray of refreshments toppling down on his head.

The other man's arrogant, aristocratic face twisted in anger at the sight of Leonardo. "Are there mice in every corner of this infernal place!" he snarled.

Flinging Fresina aside, he drew his sword. Leonardo leapt out of the chest, lunging at him. The swordsman dodged and Leonardo pitched helplessly on to his belly, the blade slashing through the air above his head.

Leonardo made an undignified scramble to get out of reach. Rodrigo, meanwhile, was struggling to pick himself up. "By Christ's wounds!" he croaked. "I saw that boy at Silvestro's. He must be a Medici spy!"

"Then he will learn that he has chosen the wrong side," said his companion. He pushed Leonardo on to his back with the toe of his boot and pointed the sword at his chest.

Leonardo stared at the blade. "I'm no spy!" he gasped. But he knew that would not save him.

Then he saw Fresina jump to her feet and seize hold of the easel. Whirling her body around like a pinwheel, she slammed Lucrezia's portrait right into the swordsman's face. The man went down like a felled ox, colliding with Rodrigo so that they both went rolling across the floor.

Leonardo jumped up and grabbed the slave girl by the arm. "Come on!"

She dropped her makeshift weapon and the two of them made a dash for the door. Once in the passage, Leonardo darted towards the stairs.

"Where are we going?" the girl asked.

"Anywhere we won't be murdered," Leonardo said.

Confused shouts and hurrying footsteps were converging from all parts of the house. Statues and hangings flew by in a blur as the two fugitives raced to the front door and tumbled out into the street. Their headlong exit turned the heads of passers by and sharp cries of alarm broke out behind them.

"Murder! Murder! Stop them!"

Heads appeared at neighbouring windows.

"That girl! Look, there's blood on her dress!" a voice cried.

"She's a slave!" exclaimed another, making it sound like an even worse accusation.

Leonardo took Fresina by the hand and yanked her around the corner of the house into a lane. It led to a maze of backstreets that were now sunk in shadow with the setting of the sun. The sounds of pursuit faded behind them. Once they were several streets away, they paused for breath.

Leonardo looked at Fresina. To his eyes the bloodstains on her robe blazed like the flames of a bonfire. "We have to get out of sight," he said.

They ducked into an alley that took them to the rear of a tavern. Here they squatted down behind a stack of barrels, safe from sight. Distant voices still barked here and there, but the general alarm was subsiding as the chase petered out.

"Why were those men trying to kill you?" Leonardo asked.

Fresina gave him a sidelong look. "If I tell you, perhaps you will try to kill me too."

"Nonsense. I saved you."

"I suppose that is true," Fresina conceded.

Leonardo was taken aback by her surly manner. "You could at least try to sound grateful."

"I am a slave," the girl retorted flatly. "People treat me however the whim takes them. What has gratitude to do with it?"

Leonardo shook his head and tried to get back to the point. "Look, I need to know what happened back there."

Fresina drummed her fingers on her knees. "I see Tomasso let them into the house by a back door. The three of them are sneaking about like thieves, so I follow. I am very good at not being seen."

"Not good enough, it seems," Leonardo observed.

Fresina showed her teeth like a vixen. "And you, you would do better? You are the one who fell on his face!" She slapped her palm flat on the ground.

Leonardo took a deep breath to calm himself. Talking to this girl was like wrestling with a cat. "What happened next?" he asked.

"Next I hear them talk nonsense, about someone called Gottoso."

"Gottoso? Who is that?"

"I do not know. Did you not listen when I said it was nonsense? Then they find me. At first I get away, but then Tomasso catches me" – she made a snatching movement with both hands – "and they pull me into that room where you are hidden like a thief."

"I am no thief," said Leonardo. "It was an accident."

"So what are we to do now? Hide here until we starve?"

Leonardo rubbed his brow. "I don't know. It's only a matter of time before the city guards come looking for us."

Fresina shuddered and her blue eyes revealed a gleam of fear. "You cannot let them take me. Last year, a slave named Lucia was accused of poisoning her master, and do you know what they did to her?"

Leonardo shook his head.

"She was hauled through the streets so everyone could spit on her. Then flesh was torn from her bones with red hot pincers before she was burned alive at the stake."

Leonardo felt his stomach heave. "And you witnessed this?"

"Every slave in the city saw it," said Fresina, her eyes glistening. "It was meant as a lesson to all of us."

"But still, the truth is on our side," said Leonardo.

"The truth!" Suddenly, Fresina was all fire again. "Who would care what I say, a runaway slave with blood on her hands?"

"They might listen to me."

"And who are you?"

"I am apprenticed to Maestro Andrea del Verrocchio, one of the most respected artists in the city."

"Artist!" Fresina spat the word out like it was a seed that had been stuck to her tongue. "Why could you not be a man of influence? A banker perhaps."

Leonardo bristled. "I am also a debt collector."

Fresina pondered this. "That is more promising," she admitted.

"Yes, but still not enough," Leonardo said. "We need to get to someone who will believe me, but we won't get far if anybody spots the blood on your clothes. You stay here while I scout around."

He stood up and made his way around to the side of the tavern. Through an open window he could see the place was filled with workmen washing away the thirst of a long day with ale and wine, and satisfying their hunger with bread and roasted meat.

The group nearest to him had cast their cloaks upon the

floor close by. They had already littered their table with empty wine jugs and had just commenced a bawdy song about a soldier and a miller's daughter.

The landlord hurried over from the bar. "Gentlemen, gentlemen, I beg you. There are some priests eating their supper at that table over there."

"Priests? Why should they worry?" joked one of the men. "They hear worse things every day in confession."

His friends all roared with laughter and they launched back into their song with fresh vigour. The landlord was still trying vainly to quiet them when Fresina appeared at Leonardo's side.

She peered inside and a sly smile lit her lips. "That is what we need."

Before Leonardo could stop her, she leaned in through the window. She stretched so far she would have fallen in if Leonardo had not caught hold of the back of her robe. She groped around until she located one of the discarded cloaks. With a hiss she wriggled back and slid down beside Leonardo, her prize bundled up in her arms.

Inside the wine shop the singing continued without interruption. Leonardo stared at the girl, aghast. "You stole that!"

"Of course. In Circassia a good thief is praised for his

nimble fingers and his daring."

Leonardo sighed. A stolen cloak, he supposed, was a small enough crime compared to what they were already accused of.

Fresina sneaked away from the window and wrapped the cloak around herself. Both the bloodstains and her distinctive slave's garb were hidden in its folds.

"There – now where do we go?"

"There's only one person I can go to," said Leonardo, "but I don't think he'll be pleased to see us."

9

The Hand of God

Maestro Andrea del Verrocchio's own apartments were above the workshop and were reached by a private stairway off the main street. At the top of the steps Leonardo paused.

"You keep quiet and let me do all the talking," he instructed Fresina.

"I hope you talk better than you fight," Fresina muttered.

Leonardo wondered whether he should have left her behind, but he dismissed the thought and knocked gently. There was a scuffle of feet and the door opened, revealing

Maestro Andrea's round face. The artist's brow furrowed.

"Leonardo da Vinci, what are you doing here?"

"I need your help, Maestro," Leonardo replied.

Andrea stepped back to admit his visitors and closed the door behind them. "Who is this girl?" he asked.

"I will explain everything to you," Leonardo promised, "but first I must tell you this – neither of us is guilty of any crime."

A strange expression passed across Andrea's face like a shadow on the moon. "You had best sit down," he said, gesturing towards a bench.

As he and Fresina seated themselves, Leonardo noted the girl's eyes darting suspiciously about the simply furnished room, as if she expected a trap to be sprung. Andrea settled himself on a chair opposite and fixed his pupil with a quizzical gaze.

"It all began with Sandro Botticelli," said Leonardo. "He wanted me to help him with a piece of work without his client, Lorenzo de' Medici, learning of my involvement. This was at the house of the Donati family. When Lorenzo de' Medici unexpectedly called on the house, I was forced to hide inside a chest. When everyone else had left, I discovered that I was locked in."

He stopped and looked up, expecting Andrea to

question him or to laugh at how ludicrous the story sounded. The artist's face was a complete blank. With a tiny movement of the head he prompted his pupil to continue.

From there on Leonardo told the whole story in as much detail as he could recall. He even admitted how he had fallen flat after leaping from the chest.

"Finally, Maestro, I could think of nowhere else to go," he concluded. "There was no one else I could trust."

Andrea leaned back and rubbed his hands on his thighs. "Your story is absurd, Leonardo."

Fresina had kept doggedly silent, but now she burst out, "If he were making this up, would he make himself out such a fool? No, he would give himself the part of a hero."

"I did risk my life for you," Leonardo reminded her, nettled by her critical words.

Andrea raised a hand to quiet them both. He said to the girl, "It is not possible to make any sense of this unless we know why these men wished to dispose of you."

Fresina made a disgusted noise. "It is as I told Leonardo, they talked nonsense."

"Why don't you tell me exactly what was said?" Andrea suggested placidly.

Fresina sprang up. The cloak slipped from her shoulders

and Andrea flinched at the sight of the blood on her dress. Oblivious to his reaction, she threw herself into her tale.

"I creep along behind them, out of sight," she began, tiptoeing across the floor. "Then I listen at the door they shut themselves behind." She cocked an ear, re-enacting the whole scene. "I do not hear all because some of them speak louder than others. Tomasso, he is the quietest, the most afraid of being heard, but he is complaining that they ask too much of him.

"'Information is all we need,' say the others. 'The comings and goings of your mistress and her friend Lorenzo.'

"Tomasso says something else. 'You are too fond of the dice and the cards,' the men say. 'You owe us very much money. What do you think will happen if we call in the debt? You will go to prison and what will become of your wife and children?'

"Tomasso is worried about someone he calls Il Gottoso. He worries what he will do."

"That is Piero de' Medici," said Andrea. "He suffers badly from gout, an inflammation of the joints that causes him great pain. That is why they call him Il Gottoso, the Gouty One."

"The other two say not to worry about him," Fresina

resumed, raising her voice to let them know she was vexed at being interrupted. "They say everything has been arranged and Il Gottoso will be struck down by the hand of God."

"God?" Leonardo repeated, puzzled.

Fresina silenced him with a scowl. "Yes, God!" she repeated emphatically. "Tomasso makes a noise like he is giving in. 'You must be ready for the signal to let our men in,' they tell him. 'We will strike like lightning and there will be no time for mistakes.' One of them laughs when they say this. I do not know why."

Leonardo was about to interrupt but Andrea signalled him to keep quiet.

"Then I lean too hard against the door," said Fresina, stumbling forward. "It falls open and I am seen. I turn and run, but they chase me down the passage. Tomasso takes hold of me and they drag me into the closest room before I can get free." She wrapped her arms around herself and wobbled from side to side. "After that Leonardo has told you all, the foolishness included."

"And you do not know who these men were?" Andrea asked. The girl shook her head. He turned to Leonardo. "Nor you?"

"One of them I saw at Silvestro's yesterday, but all I

know is that his name is Rodrigo."

Andrea got up and went to his desk. He came back with a sheet of paper and a piece of crayon which he handed to his pupil. "Draw the man who was commanding Rodrigo."

Leonardo quickly sketched the features of the two men. Fresina leaned over him, puckering her mouth. "The nose should be longer," she said.

"It is exactly correct," Leonardo retorted testily. He handed the drawing to his master.

Andrea bit his lip. "You did not recognise this man?" he asked, pointing to the aristocratic face.

"No," Leonardo replied.

Andrea tapped the picture with his finger. "He is Diotisalvi Neroni, the most dangerous man in Florence. I heard he has a mercenary in his employ, a Spaniard who acts as bodyguard and messenger for him. If Neroni is your accuser, you may as well stick your head in the noose."

"But, Maestro, what is all this about?"

Andrea sat down again and motioned to the other two to do likewise. "As you know," he began, "when the bankrupt aristocrats lost power and the trade guilds took over the running of our city, the Signoria was created, a body of nine men elected every two months from the membership of the guilds. The day to day affairs of Florence are tended by the

Signoria, but there are important decisions which cannot be left to their squabbling. That is why the real power lies with the head of the wealthy Medici family, first the great Cosimo de' Medici and now his son Piero."

"Lorenzo's father," Leonardo explained to Fresina.

"I know that!" she hissed at him.

"Since Cosimo's death," Andrea continued, "Luca Pitti, a vain buffoon who fancies himself a hero of the people, has been trying to oust the Medici and make himself our leading citizen. He has not the wit to achieve this himself, but he has a dangerous ally in Neroni. Neroni is as cunning as a fox and he knows that it is he himself who will really hold the reins of power should the Medici fall."

"What can we do against such a man?" asked Leonardo.

"Nothing," Andrea declared flatly. "All we can do is get you out of here. As soon as they learn who you are, this is the first place they will come looking for you."

"Could you not go to the Medici and tell them?" Leonardo suggested.

"Tell them what?" Andrea demanded. "That my apprentice was locked in a chest? That he has fled with a runaway slave girl and they are both accused of murder? And what will become of me, do you think, if it ever comes out that I had a hand in helping you?"

Leonardo hung his head. Until now he had not thought of just how much trouble he was bringing down on his master. "I am sorry. There was nowhere else."

Andrea huffed for a moment and then spoke in a more sympathetic tone. "What we must do is get you out of the city before the Constable's men find you here."

The next instant all three of them started in fright. As if in answer to Andrea's words, there was an urgent banging at the door.

10

The Outcasts of Heaven

Andrea stood bolt upright. Inhaling sharply between clenched teeth, he waved Leonardo and Fresina to a corner out of sight. The banging grew louder. Taking a moment to straighten his tunic and restore his composure, Andrea walked up to the door and opened it.

Sandro Botticelli almost fell headlong into the room.

"Andrea," he gasped, "have you seen Leonardo? I looked for him among the apprentices downstairs but—"

Andrea yanked him into the centre of the room and slammed the door shut. As soon as he glimpsed Leonardo lurking in the corner Sandro raised his eyes to Heaven with hands outspread. "May all the saints be thanked!" he exclaimed.

"Sandro!" Leonardo cried, running to clasp his friend's hand.

When they had released each other, Sandro caught sight of Fresina emerging from the shadows. "You've brought the murderess here!" he exclaimed. "Are you mad?"

"She's no more a killer than I am," said Leonardo. "But tell me, what are you doing here?"

"We got to the dinner party at Alberti's house and – can you believe it? – I was seated at the very lowest part of the table between some Greek silk trader who barely spoke a word of Italian and a fish merchant with bad breath. Fine clients they would make for an aspiring artist!"

"Sandro, we do not have much time," Andrea pressed him.

"Yes, of course," said Sandro. "I was still thinking of Leonardo back at the Donati house, hoping he had managed to get out without ruining our plan. I made an excuse and left Alberti's, intending to gain entry to the Torre Donati by claiming I had returned for some brushes I had left behind. When I got there the whole street was in uproar. I was told that the chamberlain had been murdered by a slave girl, who had then fled with an unidentified youth."

"Unidentified – what a relief!" said Leonardo.

"It won't be long before they find out who you are," said Sandro. "All they have to do is ask Lucrezia Donati." He groaned. "How could you get into such a mess? What happened to the man Tomasso?"

"It was two other men who killed him," Leonardo replied. "They made it look as though Fresina had committed the crime and they planned to do away with her as well. I explained it all to Maestro Andrea."

Andrea was pacing the floor in long strides, clenching and unclenching his fists. Catching Sandro's eye, he said, "We all know the penalty for aiding an escaped slave is death, but we cannot worry about that. Even as we speak the city gates are being closed, so the only way out is by the river."

"My father has a rowboat," said Sandro. "He keeps it tied up by the tannery, close to the water. He used to use it a lot, but now he—"

Andrea stopped him short with a jab of his finger. "Go and fetch it as quickly as you can. We will meet you beneath the Ponte alle Grazia, here on the north side of the river."

He bundled the young artist outside and shut the door after him. Then he turned to Fresina and rubbed his jaw like a man plagued by a toothache.

"You cannot go around in that bloodstained dress. We will have to find you some other clothes. Perhaps we could borrow an outfit from one of the apprentices."

Soon they were hurrying through the streets towards the river. Fresina was dressed in a tunic and breeches with her long, fair hair bunched up under a round cap. The stolen cloak was wrapped around her slender shoulders.

"It's lucky Gabriello is close to her size," said Leonardo.

"I'll buy him a fresh suit of clothes to replace these," said Andrea.

Fresina sniffed at her sleeve. "They are not even clean."

"I had to take them out of the laundry pile so no one would notice," said Leonardo. "I didn't think a slave would be so fussy."

"My mistress always insists my clothes are clean and spotless," said Fresina proudly. "The Donati keep a very fine house."

"Then why don't you go back to the Donati?" snapped

Leonardo. "Obviously nothing I've done is good enough for you."

Fresina's lip quivered. Averting her face she hurried on ahead. Leonardo felt ashamed of himself for lashing out at her. He started to catch up, but Andrea laid a hand on his shoulder.

"Let her cry her tears now and get them out of the way."

By now they had reached the river's edge. A slippery path took them down under the Ponte alle Grazia, which was the closest bridge to the workshop.

The water lapped quietly against the stonework, and here and there the dark shape of a boat slid silently down the river. Chapels had been built upon the piers that thrust out from the bridge and from them came the rhythmic murmur of worshippers at their evening prayers. Fresina slumped into a heap in the shadows, her face buried in her folded arms.

"Maestro," Leonardo began, "I know how much trouble I am bringing down upon you, but..."

Andrea waved the apology aside. "I do it for myself because I too was once unjustly accused," he said gruffly. Then he added, "And I do it for you... because you have it in you to one day be a great artist."

Leonardo was taken aback. It was the first compliment

Andrea had ever paid him. "Really, Maestro?"

"Do you think I would have tolerated you this long if I did not believe that?"

"But I thought Nicolo was your favourite. You allow him to do real art while I wash brushes and prepare canvas."

"I encourage him to practise his technique, for although it is a pale imitation of my own, it is all he will ever have. From you I expect more. I expect you to find something inside yourself that will make you both a great artist and a great man. Everything else follows from that."

"That's what I want too, Maestro."

"No, Leonardo, what you want is success, fame and wealth. But those are not the things that make a man great."

"I don't understand."

"Let me tell you a story that someone once told to me," said Andrea. He gazed out over the surface of the river, as if he could see pictures forming there. "Long ago, at the beginning of the world, when Satan in his pride rebelled against God, there were angels who were too cowardly to join either side. They thought only of themselves and hid from the war in Heaven.

"Afterwards, as they were neither good enough for Heaven nor wicked enough for Hell, God took away their wings and exiled them to earth. Here they became the souls of men, and only by proving their courage can they regain their wings. That is what makes us great, Leonardo, our choices and the courage we need to make them."

Leonardo fell silent. For the first time he realised how little he had understood of what his master had been trying to teach him ever since he arrived in Florence.

Fresina's voice suddenly piped up. "The boat!"

She jumped to her feet, her spirits instantly restored.

Andrea frowned. "Is it Sandro?"

Leonardo's keen eyes peered through the gloom. "Yes, it is." He waved and Sandro returned his salute before bringing the boat to rest beneath the bridge. Sandro's face bore signs of strain and Leonardo felt a pang of conscience: it must have been very hard for him to row this far with an injured wrist.

"Get in quickly!" Sandro urged breathlessly.

He helped Fresina and Leonardo climb aboard but when Sandro tried to sit down again, Leonardo hauled him up by the arm.

"You stay here, Sandro. We will go the rest of the way ourselves."

"But how will my father get his boat back?"

"Don't worry about that," said Leonardo grimly. "Worry

about what will happen to you if you are caught helping us."

"Leonardo is right," Andrea said, offering his hand. "You have done all you can."

He helped Sandro ashore then pushed the boat away from the bank. Sandro gave a wave of farewell before Andrea dragged him off. As he watched them disappear, Leonardo realised that he was not so alone as he had always thought. But the knowledge may have come too late: he did not know if he would ever see Andrea and Sandro again.

He turned the boat around and started westward, keeping close to the shore so they could hide in the shadows. Only when he looked back and saw the walls of Florence slipping into the darkness behind them did he begin to relax.

"We should be safe now," he said. "With any luck they won't guess we've managed to escape the city."

"There is no escape for me," said Fresina. "Wherever I go, I am still a slave and I will be hunted."

Leonardo adjusted their course to avoid a sandbank. "How did you become a slave?" he asked after a long silence. "Were you convicted of a crime or captured in war?"

"My father needed money. So he sold me."

"Your father?" Leonardo was shocked.

Fresina shrugged. "It is common enough. After all, a daughter cannot fight in battle or plough a field. He told me I was going to become an important lady in the palace of a Turkish sultan. Instead, I was packed into a cramped, smelly ship with a hundred other slaves, many of them younger than me."

She rubbed a hand across her eyes and continued. "We sailed, I do not know for how long. There is no night and day in the darkness below decks. At last I was brought to the city of Venice and locked up there. I was given short but intense lessons in the Italian tongue and the Christian faith – so that I would fetch a better price."

"You must hate your father," Leonardo said.

Fresina's face was invisible in the dark. "He had to think of the good of the family," she said. "We Circassians are a practical people."

"I think perhaps we are not so very different from each other after all," Leonardo murmured.

"You still have not told me where we are going," said Fresina. "Are you just going to row and row until somebody stops us?"

"I'm taking you home," Leonardo grunted between strokes of the oars.

Fresina leapt up with a squeak, almost overbalancing the boat. Leonardo gripped the side to keep himself from falling overboard and waved her angrily back to her seat.

"Sit down, you silly little fool! You almost capsized us!"

Fresina sat back down with a defiant glower. "Why are you so afraid? Can you not swim?"

Leonardo realised his hand was trembling. With an effort of will he managed to steady it. "Of course I can swim," he snapped. "But there are treacherous currents in this river that can suck you under unexpectedly. A man would have to be able to breathe underwater to survive them."

Fresina narrowed her eyes, realising that she had given him a genuine scare. "I will sit still if you wish," she said, "but do you really think you can reach Circassia in this boat?"

"Don't be ridiculous," said Leonardo. "I'm taking you to *my* home. To Anchiano."

"Oh," said Fresina, her shoulders sagging.

"Believe me," Leonardo told her, "I'd much rather we were going to Circassia, no matter how far away it is. We'd probably get a warmer welcome there."

11

The Homecoming

The next day even the landscape seemed to bear out the truth of Leonardo's words. It was not very welcoming.

"How many more hills must we climb?" Fresina complained, flinging herself down on the grass. "I swear we could have walked to Circassia by now."

Leonardo did his best to be patient. "We've come most of the way by boat," he said, "and it's only a few more miles on foot."

He had tied the boat up in the night so they could catch a few hours' sleep. They had resumed their journey with the dawn, following the Arno westward to where it would eventually reach the port of Pisa and the waters of the Tyrrhenian Sea. An hour ago they pulled into shore close to the town of Empoli and concealed the boat beneath some overhanging bushes. Leonardo knew they might need it again, depending on what happened when they reached Anchiano.

He sat down beside the girl, his eyes following a hawk as it sailed effortlessly across the blue sky.

"Why are you always watching the birds?" Fresina asked suspiciously. "Are you looking for omens?"

"I don't believe in omens," said Leonardo. "I want to understand how birds fly."

"And why do you want to know that?"

"When I was only an infant, a bird – a kite it was – landed in my cot. It hopped on to my chest then tickled my nose with its tail feathers before flying away. I stretched out my arms and howled because I couldn't fly after it."

"And that is why you watch the birds – because you want to fly after them?"

"I suppose so."

Fresina nodded knowingly. "You want to be a sorcerer then."

"Of course not. Only fools believe in magic."

"How can a man fly without magic?" Fresina

demanded, waving her fingers under his nose. "He cannot fly unless he first tames the spirits of air."

"The spirits of air?"

Fresina scowled at his ignorance. "Back in Circassia we have wizards who know of such things. They summon the spirits of air to bring the wind and the spirits of water to bring rain. Of course, now that I am a Christian..." she made a perfunctory sign of the cross over her breast "...I no longer believe in such things."

"I believe in the things I can see, the things I can touch," said Leonardo. "A bird, by the action of its wings, moves through the air the way a fish swims in water. So why can't a man do the same?"

"Because he has no wings," said Fresina. "You can no more fly with the birds than I can sit at table with my mistress."

"I would need to build something," Leonardo admitted. "Wings of leather or wickerwork perhaps." Suddenly, he could see himself soaring over the green hills of Tuscany with a huge pair of man-made wings strapped to his back.

Fresina squinted at him critically. "You are a fool if you will not use magic. The men who are trying to kill us are sorcerers and only magic can protect us from them." She spat on her forefinger and smeared an invisible symbol on her brow. "If you have any sense, you too will make a mark against the evil eye."

Leonardo roused from his reverie. "What makes you think they're sorcerers?"

Fresina almost snarled with impatience. "Did I not tell you what they said? They are going to summon the hand of God to destroy their enemies, just like the sorcerers in my own land. In Circassia they call upon Shible for thunder, Tleps for fire and Seosseres for wind."

"You need to leave those superstitions behind," said Leonardo. "All they do is muddle the mind. Do you talk this way to your master and mistress?"

Fresina swallowed suddenly and seized him by the hand. "You must swear to tell no one I spoke of these things," she said urgently. "I am a good Christian now and I would be beaten if my master, Signor Donati, knew I had spoken of heathen things."

"I won't tell anyone," Leonardo promised. "But this has nothing to do with magic. It's something to do with a machine."

Fresina wrinkled her face at him as though he were raving.

"Never mind," Leonardo sighed. "That knowledge won't do us any good now." He had meant to show the drawing to Maestro Andrea, but events had moved too quickly. And Anchiano was the last place on earth where he could expect such mysteries to be solved.

Overhead, the hawk swooped down on an unsuspecting sparrow and snatched it away in its sharp claws. The ruthlessness of the kill reminded Leonardo of how the man Rodrigo had slain Tomasso with one thrust of his dagger.

He stood up and offered Fresina his hand. "Come on. We must not delay."

Peasants were out among the vineyards and orchards, chatting as they worked. Knowing all the paths and tracks of the region, Leonardo was able to keep his distance from them to ensure he was not recognised.

"You say your family has a farm here?" said Fresina.

"Yes, up there on the slopes of Monte Albano," said Leonardo, pointing to the high ground ahead. "Vinci, the town we take our family name from, is on the other side of the mountain. Most of our fields are hired out to peasant farmers who pay a share of their crop as rent to my grandfather Antonio."

"And your father lives here also?"

"Sometimes," Leonardo answered uncomfortably. "He's a notary."

"What is that?"

"He draws up business contracts and arranges the sale of land and property," Leonardo explained. "He travels a lot because of his work."

"But your mother will be here."

"No, she will not," Leonardo responded sharply.

Fresina flinched at the harshness of his tone. She eyed him curiously. "Then who is there to help us?"

"My grandparents are kindly people," Leonardo explained. "They may find us a place to hide until this business is cleared up."

He broke off at the sight of a familiar figure ahead and a happy smile drove the trouble from his face. A rugged, wide-shouldered man with thick curly hair was striding towards them, carrying a pitchfork in one hand. Leonardo waved eagerly.

"Who is this?" Fresina asked.

"It's my uncle!" Leonardo exclaimed. "Uncle Francesco!"

He ran to the man and the two embraced. By the time Fresina had caught up, Leonardo had become sober again. "Is my father here?" he asked.

The welcoming grin faded from Francesco da Vinci's plain, guileless face. "He's in Pistoia on business. Don't expect him back before tomorrow."

"And is *she* with him?"

"She is," Francesco replied.

"That's good," said Leonardo. "I wouldn't want him involved. Not with his reputation."

"Involved in what?" asked Francesco. He raised an eyebrow as he looked at Fresina. "And who is this?"

"Fresina, the reason I'm here," said Leonardo. "We had to get out of Florence to escape some powerful men."

Francesco's brow creased like a newly ploughed field and he worked his lips as if he were digesting a difficult meal. "It sounds complicated," he said. "You can explain when we get home."

He strode off up the winding path and Leonardo and Fresina followed behind.

"He talks younger than he looks," Fresina observed in a whisper.

"He has a good heart," Leonardo said defensively, "even though my father treats him like a fool."

Soon they came to a large cottage surrounded by several smaller outbuildings. Franceso paused. "Best the girl stays out here till we talk to your grandfather," he said.

Leonardo agreed. "Fresina, you stay out of sight by that wagon over there. I'll come for you shortly."

He followed Franceso indoors to a plain room with a large hearth, a simple rug and one hanging on the wall showing a scene of a horse race. The old man seated by the fireplace stood up shakily. A weak smile shone through his thick white beard.

"Leonardo!" he said. "My boy, how have you been?"

"Well, Grandfather," Leonardo replied, embracing the old man.

"Your grandmother will be overjoyed," said the aged Ser Antonio da Vinci. "She misses you greatly. Even more than Francesco misses your help on the farm."

"Wait till I show you the new calves, Leonardo," Francesco beamed.

Leonardo was about to speak, but was struck dumb when another man emerged from the back of the house. He was tall and handsome and dressed in a fine brocaded doublet. Behind him was a pretty young woman, only a few years older than Leonardo, whose head was bowed in wifely submission.

"Piero, what are you doing here?" Francesco exclaimed. "I thought you were in Pistoia."

"My business concluded early," replied Piero da Vinci. "More to the point, what is my son doing here?" He turned a baleful eye upon Leonardo.

12

The Prodigal Son

If he had been dragged in chains before the magistrates of Florence, Leonardo could not have felt more guilty. His throat went dry and he had to cough before he could speak. The last thing he could do now was tell the truth.

"Hello, Father," he said lamely. "I had a few days free so I thought I would come home."

His father's proud lips curled. "To do what exactly? To almost drown in the river again? To fill the house with lizards and insects?"

"They were models for his drawing," said Francesco. "And very fine monsters he made out of them too."

"That is why he belongs with Andrea del Verrocchio," said Ser Piero. "To turn that idle scribbling into a proper profession. He shows little enough aptitude for the law or for farming." He fixed a suspicious eye on Leonardo. "Why should Andrea allow you to go? Today is no holiday that I know of."

"Things are very slow at the workshop," Leonardo said, knowing how feeble this sounded.

"You aren't in some sort of trouble again, are you?" Ser Piero asked accusingly. "I told Andrea to keep a sharp eye on you. I warned him of how undisciplined you are."

Leonardo shuffled his feet and could not meet his father's eyes. "No, that's not it at all."

"Then why are you here? What are you hiding?"

Leonardo knew he had to come up with a reason his father would accept without question and he could think of only one. He looked up and spoke clearly.

"I came to ask for money."

"Ha! I thought as much!" said Ser Piero, raising a hand in the air as though he had just scored a point in court. "Did I not negotiate a salary for you with Andrea? Did I not give you enough to equip yourself for your new career?"

"Life in Florence is very expensive," said Leonardo petulantly. He knew that the worse he made himself appear in his father's eyes, the less chance there was his father would question his reasons for being in Anchiano.

"What is expensive? Fine clothes? The best wine? That is not what I sent you there for."

"I must make an appearance of being a gentleman," said Leonardo. "I would not want to shame you."

"Shame me? If you are neglecting your studies to come here begging for money, then that is exactly what you are doing."

Ser Antonio tried to intervene. "Piero, I am sure he will not be staying long. We could spare him something."

"Do not let him take advantage of your soft heart, Father," said Piero. "He does not even have the manners to greet his mother properly."

He ushered his young bride forward. The girl looked embarrassed, but did her best to smile upon her stepson. Leonardo bowed his head.

"Piero, he has come a long way," said Francesco mildly. "We should offer him a meal."

"There is food for him in Florence," growled Piero. "Maestro Andrea does not let his apprentices starve, even if he does not dress them up in silk and gold."

Leonardo's eyes were smarting. This had all gone horribly wrong. "I was a fool to come here," he said.

Before his father could voice his agreement, he turned on his heel and dashed out of the door. He stopped outside and rested his back against the wall as he fought to control his sobbing. When he looked up he was astonished to see his father had followed him.

"Are you in some sort of trouble, Leonardo?" Piero's tone had softened, but it was still an accusation.

"If I were, what difference would it make to you?" Leonardo flung the words at him like a handful of stones.

"I was worried for you. I still remember the day you ran off and threw yourself into the river."

"That's not what happened. You don't understand."

"Well, in spite of what you did, in spite of what you said to me, we are both alive still. But your life won't amount to much unless you take command of it."

"I thought it was you who commanded my life."

"I have done you a favour," his father said, stern once more. "I have given you a way to turn these fancies of yours to profit. But it will still take effort on your part."

Leonardo looked pointedly away, but his father kept talking.

"Do you see, when I walk down the street, how the people bow their heads and address me in terms of deepest respect? Such a prominent position has to be earned. It takes years of hard work."

The words stung Leonardo. He knew that what he hoped to gain by helping the Medici was just the sort of respect his father was talking about, and that just made everything worse.

"Is that all you want from me then, that I should go back to Florence and drudge in a workshop?" he demanded angrily.

"I want you to take responsibility for yourself," his father retorted with equal rage, "not to just run away from a challenge."

Leonardo's stomach was churning and he could think of nothing else to say. He ran off down the path and lost himself among the olive trees. After a short while Fresina appeared beside him.

"I was hiding behind a barrel outside the house," she said. "I heard it all. I followed as soon as your father went inside."

Flushed with embarrassment, Leonardo grabbed her by the arm and dragged her off down the path after him. "We can't stay here," he told her in a cracked voice.

"Then where are we to go?" she protested. "We are almost out of food."

"I don't care," snapped Leonardo, shepherding her

down the hill. "I'd rather starve than go back there."

"Your father will not help you?" Fresina asked.

"He has his reputation to think of," said Leonardo bitterly. "That is all he values, that and the next pretty face he takes a fancy to. If he knew I was in trouble with the law, he would beat me soundly before handing me over to the magistrates."

Fresina sighed. "So we came here for nothing."

"There is one place left to go," said Leonardo. "And in its own way it's as dangerous as going back to Florence."

A half hour's walk brought them to the hillside overlooking the village of Campo Zeppi.

"You say your mother lives here?" said Fresina.

"She was a peasant girl my father took a fancy to in his youth," Leonardo explained grudgingly. "Even when she bore him a child, it was impossible for an important man like him to marry someone so lowly. She was allowed to nurse me for the first year of my life, but as soon as he found a more suitable bride, he sent her away. And when that well-born wife died childless last year, he quickly married another to bring him a legitimate heir."

He looked away so that the girl would not see the misery in his face. Fresina touched him tentatively on the shoulder. "You don't have to hide your pain from me. I know what it is to be taken from your mother."

Suddenly, Leonardo dropped into a crouch behind some shrubs, pulling Fresina down beside him.

"What is it?" she asked nervously.

"Down there, the road beyond the village," Leonardo said. He pointed to a rider mounted on a chestnut gelding who was trotting around the hill, his back turned towards them.

"Do you know him?" Fresina asked.

"I can't see his face, but I'm sure he's not from around here," Leonardo replied.

They waited until the horseman had passed out of sight behind a grove of poplars before emerging from hiding.

"It was just a man on a horse," said Fresina. "You act like he was an evil spirit."

"Never mind," said Leonardo, glancing to where the sun was sinking behind the hills. "We must get to Caterina's before dark."

An hour later they came in sight of a rough, stone-built cottage on the edge of the village. Fresina gazed upon the squalid dwelling with distaste. "It's very small. Does your mother live here alone?"

"No, she married a long time ago," Leonardo replied. "Her husband is a lime burner named Tonio, though everybody calls him the Brawler. You'll find out why."

They continued walking down the dirt track and had almost reached the cottage when a chorus of squeals erupted from inside. Four children of various ages – a boy and three girls – came pouring out the door, chasing each other and squeaking with excitement. The boy was the youngest and he was swatting one of the girls with a stick.

"Maffeo, leave Madalena alone!" a woman's voice shouted after him.

She emerged into the light, the children scattering like a flock of starlings before her. As soon as she caught sight of Leonardo she pulled up short and wiped some dust from the front of her apron. She was a pretty woman in her early thirties, her long brown hair held back from her sun-browned face by a plain white kerchief that was knotted behind her head.

She placed her hands on her hips and regarded the boy.

"Leonardo, it's been a long time," she said, arching an eyebrow. She spoke in the clipped accent of rural Tuscany.

"Caterina," Leonardo answered. His hands were twitching nervously, as if he wanted to reach out to her, but was afraid to do so.

Caterina clucked her tongue. "Leonardo, you can call me Mother here." She made an exaggerated show of looking all round her. "We're not in church or the market where someone might overhear."

Leonardo glanced round about at the hillside and the nearby cottages. His caution was genuine for he remembered the horseman. "Can we go inside?"

Caterina stood where she was, blocking the entrance. "Who is your friend," she asked, "and why is she dressed as a boy?"

"These were the only clothes we could find for her," Leonardo replied.

Caterina scrutinised Fresina in a way that was curious but not unfriendly. She tilted her head towards the cottage and led the way inside.

Only a few shafts of light penetrated the small windows, illuminating a single room with a hearth at one end and some piles of folded blankets at the other. In the middle of the room was a wooden table surrounded by a circle of stools. Along the walls were shelves filled with clay pots and cooking utensils.

Caterina motioned her visitors to be seated at the table while she laid out some bread and fetched a pitcher of water. "You look like you've been travelling," she said as she sat down on a stool and poured the water.

Fresina drank thirstily and bobbed her head in thanks.

"We've come all the way from Florence," she said.

"What? Just to see me?" Caterina joked.

"To ask for your help," said Leonardo. "We need a place to hide for a few days."

"And you thought this would be a good place?" His mother waved her hand around at the bare walls. "I suppose your father would not help?"

Leonardo did not reply.

Caterina laughed. "No, he wouldn't, would he? So you are in trouble." She looked Fresina in the eye. "Is that right?"

Fresina nodded. "I don't know that hiding is going to help us."

Leonardo sensed that this was a slight against him. "It's the only plan I have for now," he said testily.

"And who are you, girl?" Caterina asked, keeping her gaze fixed steadily on Fresina.

"She's a servant," Leonardo interjected hastily. "There was some trouble in the house where she works, but she is innocent of any wrongdoing."

"Is that so?" Caterina queried sceptically. "Look at her face, hear the way she speaks. She is not from Tuscany, not even from Italy. And she has no proper clothes to wear. She is a slave."

His mother stood up and slammed her hand down on the table right in front of Leonardo. "Do you know what will happen to us if an escaped slave is found in our house?"

13

The Brawler

Leonardo could not meet his mother's stern gaze. He said woodenly, "All I know is, if we had stayed in Florence, she would be dead now and so would I."

He felt Caterina's work-hardened fingers under his chin, forcing him to look into her face. "And what is she to you?" his mother asked.

"She's just someone who needs help," Leonardo answered. "She overheard some men plotting against her master's family. They killed a man and pinned the crime on her. I was there and helped her flee, so now those men are after us both."

"What are they? Thieves?"

"Worse than that," replied Leonardo. "They are among the richest and most powerful men in Florence."

"And you defied them to help this slave girl?" said Caterina. She moved her hand from his chin and ruffled his hair approvingly. "Sometimes you still act like my son, no matter what your father has done to you."

She walked over to Fresina and laid a sympathetic hand on her arm. "The wealthy men of Florence buy these girls to be their playthings as well as their servants. And if their wives object, they soothe their injured feelings with expensive gifts of dresses and jewels. Here in the country our wealthy men have no slaves, but they still have their pleasures."

"Can we stay?" Leonardo pleaded.

Caterina sighed. "How little I see of you, my son, and when you do come, it is to place my other children and my husband in deadly danger."

"I would see you more often if I could," said Leonardo. Even to his own ears this excuse sounded weak. "But it is difficult. And right now I need your help."

There was a shrill uproar outside and cries of, "Daddy! Daddy!"

"Tonio," said Caterina. "You let me talk to him," she warned sternly.

An immense figure ducked under the doorway and for a moment it looked like he might be stuck there. Then he emerged into the room and seemed to halve its size by his mere presence.

"Caterina, I am hungry," he announced, as though it were the most important news in the world.

The Brawler spent his days shovelling limestone into a furnace. In this way they produced quicklime which was mixed with sand and water to make building mortar. In times of plague, quicklime was used to destroy the bodies of the dead. The sulphurous smell of the stuff clung to the big man as he approached the table and regarded his visitors.

Leonardo stood up respectfully and Fresina followed his lead.

The Brawler frowned. "I know this boy," he said.

"It is Leonardo," said Caterina.

"Hello, Brawler," said Leonardo, bowing his head.

The Brawler wagged a thick finger. "You should visit your mother more often, boy," he chided. "Don't you know that she—"

Caterina hushed him. "It is enough that he is here now, Tonio."

"Very well," the Brawler agreed gruffly, "but you know how I feel about a man who disrespects his mother." He clenched his fist by way of illustration. Then he squinted at Fresina. "Who is this other boy? I don't know him."

"It is a girl," said Caterina. She appeared to consider a moment before reaching a decision. "She is a slave. Leonardo brought her."

"We can't afford to keep a slave," Brawler grumbled. "Send her back."

"I'm not giving her to you," said Leonardo. "We just need a place to stay for a while."

"She is in trouble and she is being pursued by wicked men," Caterina told him bluntly.

"As they chased us, they were cursing the name of the Blessed Virgin," Leonardo added.

The Brawler's eyes flared with a sudden righteous rage. He ground his fists together like a pair of millstones.

"If a man speaks disrespectfully of the Blessed Virgin, he tastes my fist!" he growled. "If a man blasphemes against God, he tastes my fist! If a man does not venerate the saints as he should, he tastes my fist!"

Fresina pressed her lips to Leonardo's ear. "He is a very holy man," she whispered.

"No," Leonardo whispered back, "he's just a man who enjoys a good fight."

"They need a place to stay where they will be safe," said

Caterina, "until the trouble passes."

The Brawler pondered a moment. "They could stay here, as long as they share our burdens."

"I am used to doing housework," Fresina said.

"Of course, we'll do whatever we can to be useful," said Leonardo.

"It's settled then," the Brawler concluded, as though he had wrapped up all of his business for the day. "Now, when do we eat?"

Once they were gathered round the supper table a glance from their father made the boisterous children fall quiet and bow their heads. The Brawler said a grace that sounded more like a call to battle than a prayer, then they all ate hungrily.

After the meal Caterina tucked her little ones into their beds of straw, then sat down at the hearth beside Leonardo. "I heard your father had sent you to Florence to be an artist."

"He never cared for my drawings," Leonardo recalled. "Then one day, a peasant who works on our farm arrived with two rabbits he had snared. He was a good hunter and he was usually paid in coin for the game he brought. This time, however, he recognised his own cottage in one of my drawings. He said he would take that in payment for the rabbits instead of money."

He noticed that the Brawler was paying no attention to his tale. The big man was seated in the corner carving a simple doll from a piece of wood. He held it at arm's length and admired the crude strokes that were meant to represent the eyes and mouth. Leonardo wondered absently which of the children this gift was intended for.

"So what happened then?" Caterina prompted.

"When my father found out about this, he took me to see Maestro Andrea del Verrocchio in the city and showed him my drawings."

"And he was impressed?"

"If he was, he didn't show it," said Leonardo. "He just told my father that if I came to work and study with him he would pay me an allowance of four *lira* per week. Anything else would have to be provided by my family or by my own efforts. My father accepted the offer. And so got me out of the way of his new wife."

Caterina spat into the fire. "It is not just slaves who are bought and sold," she observed. "You say you came by boat?"

"Yes, I tied it up under the shelter of some trees."

"If they are looking for you, they will find it," Caterina stated decisively. "First thing in the morning, you must go down to the river and set it adrift."

Leonardo shifted uneasily. "Father knows that I have returned to Anchiano, though I did not stay in his house long. I told him I had come for money and then I ran off."

Caterina laughed and waved aside his concern. "It will never occur to him that you came here."

"It wouldn't have occurred to me either before today," said Leonardo.

"And why not?" Caterina demanded, her eyes flaring. "Are you too proud to enter your mother's poor house?"

Leonardo bowed his head, conscious of a new humility. "No," he said softly, "it's because I have no right to ask you for anything."

A long silence passed between them before Caterina spoke. "Yes, you do," she told him firmly. "You are my son."

Leonardo and Fresina were given a sleeping space and some straw to soften the packed earth floor beneath them. As silence descended upon the house, Leonardo wrapped his thin blanket around himself.

He felt Fresina edging closer to him. "Your mother is much like you," she said.

"What do you mean?"

"Her eyes. They see what is really there."

"Is it true what she said?" Leonardo asked her in a low voice.

"Is what true?"

"That your master bought you to be his... plaything?"

Fresina rolled away from him and pulled the threadbare blanket over her head. "A slave must be many things," he heard her mutter, "and she cannot complain of any of it. My young mistress, Lucrezia, she took me for her maid to keep me from her father. I think kindly of her for that."

Leonardo heard an uncharacteristic hint of gratitude in the girl's voice.

As he drifted off to sleep, Leonardo remembered the day last year when his first stepmother, Albiera, had died of a fever. His father had ordered him to cease his weeping and behave like a man. Unable to control his tears, Leonardo rushed from the house to stand on the rocky promontory that hung out over the River Arno, wishing he could escape his pain.

And now he dreamed he was spreading his arms like wings to fly away to some far-off land. Then, suddenly, the rocky edge crumbled beneath his feet and he went tumbling down into the water. The waves closed over his head and the current roared in his ears like a ravenous beast.

He awoke with a frightened gasp and gazed around the dark room. The awful noise thundered on and for an instant Leonardo thought they must be in the path of an approaching landslide. Then he realised it was just the Brawler snoring. No one else appeared to have been disturbed and he supposed they had become used to the din, just as they had accustomed themselves to so many other hardships. Fresina also slumbered on, too exhausted to be woken.

Leonardo lay down and drifted back to sleep, this time free of dreams.

There were still stars showing dimly through the windows when Caterina shook Leonardo gently awake. She led him to the table where she had already laid out a breakfast of bread, milk and fresh fruit.

"It's best you go quickly," she advised while he was eating. "Once you've set the boat loose, hurry back and keep out of sight as much as you can."

Leonardo wolfed down his breakfast before anyone else awoke. Caterina saw him out of the door. She pushed back his hair and kissed him on the brow, just as she had done with her other children.

Leonardo felt his face redden. He gave her an impulsive peck on the cheek and hurried off down the track.

It was taking the sun a long time to find its way up over the hills and there were still only a few stray shafts of light breaking the darkness of the sky. After about twenty minutes Leonardo found that he had lost his bearings. Stifling a yawn, he looked around for a landmark.

As quick as a snake, a figure stepped out of the shadows behind him and pinned his arms in a determined grip. Leonardo felt the cold touch of sharpened steel at his throat.

"Where is the girl?" rasped a chillingly familiar voice. "Tell me or by Christ's wounds, I will kill you!"

14

Dagger's Point

Leonardo knew at once that it was Rodrigo, the Spaniard he had already seen murder a man in cold blood at the Torre Donati. He swallowed hard and tried to hold his nerve.

"I don't know where she is," he answered. His voice sounded small and far away.

The pressure increased, prickling Leonardo's throat like the touch of a nettle. He felt a bead of blood trickling down towards his collar.

"I never ask a question more than once," said Rodrigo.

"We got separated," said Leonardo. "I think she ran off

towards the church of San Marco."

"You think?" the Spaniard echoed acidly. "Do you know what I think? I think I will kill you now and go looking for her by myself."

Leonardo tensed in anticipation of the blade cutting his throat, his head spinning with fear. He tried desperately to control his thoughts, but it was like trying to herd a flock of frightened sheep along the edge of a precipice.

"You're right," he gasped. "She is here and I can lead you to her."

With a satisfied grunt Rodrigo removed the blade from Leonardo's neck and released him. Leonardo lurched away, clutching his throat and panting with relief.

"So where is she hiding?" the Spaniard asked.

"In a cottage. I'll point it out for you, sir." Leonardo's voice was quavering, but in spite of his fear he was forming a plan.

He knew that as soon as he found Fresina, the Spaniard would kill them both as easily as a man swats a fly. If he fought back and forced the Spaniard to kill him now, Caterina and her family would be unaware of the danger that was stalking them. It was only a matter of time before Rodrigo found them. But perhaps there was a way to turn the tables.

"Before we collect our runaway slave," said Rodrigo, "I have a lesson for you." He displayed his hands, both empty. Then he pointed to a tree about five yards away. "Do you see that knothole halfway up the trunk?"

Leonardo nodded mutely. He saw Rodrigo's left eye narrow a fraction.

There was a metallic flash. As if from nowhere, a slender throwing knife buried itself up to the hilt right in the middle of the target. The Spaniard sauntered casually over to the tree and retrieved the weapon.

"If you try to run off or cross me in any way, I will put that blade in your heart before you can blink," he threatened. He stood before Leonardo and fixed his cold gaze upon him. "Do you understand?"

"Yes. I do, sir," Leonardo responded meekly. "I'll do whatever you say."

"Good. Then follow me."

As he trailed his captor through the trees, Leonardo tried to detect some weakness in his enemy that he might exploit. He recalled the contemptuous look the Spaniard had given him when they first met in Silvestro's workshop. Yes, he had made it clear then that he regarded Leonardo as no threat at all. If he had a weakness, it was his arrogance.

They came to a hollow where the chestnut gelding was tethered. Rodrigo unhooked a water flask from the saddle and took three swallows. Then he splashed water over his face to refresh himself.

Leonardo stroked the horse's sleek neck. The animal turned its head and nuzzled against his ear, making him smile in spite of his predicament.

"The beast is too friendly for my liking," said Rodrigo.

"I've got a way with animals, sir," said Leonardo, rubbing the horse's muzzle. "Always have."

He was doing his best to speak in the rustic accents he had worked so hard to rid himself of. He needed to convince Rodrigo that he was a simple country boy, who would not even think of defying him.

The Spaniard wiped the droplets of water from his face. "Now take me to the slave," he commanded.

"Are you taking us back to stand trial?" Leonardo asked, as he led the way to Campo Zeppi.

"Yes, that's it," said Rodrigo. "I'm going to hand you over to the Constable." He did not even try to sound convincing.

"That's good," said Leonardo with a slow nod. "She was afraid even when I told her there was no reason. It was smart of you to find me, sir."

"Silvestro had your name and that took me to

Verrocchio's workshop," Rodrigo explained with cool satisfaction. "One of your fellow apprentices was only too happy to tell me where you came from, once I had let him dip his hand into my purse."

Leonardo's fist clenched. He had no doubt that it was Nicolo who had betrayed him. That was something else to pay him back for.

"The da Vinci family is well known in these parts," Rodrigo continued. "I kept watch over your family home and last night I investigated it while they were all asleep."

"You must be as quiet as a cat, sir," said Leonardo, allowing his voice to shake.

"When I found you were not there, I decided to lie in wait on the main track from Empoli and the river. I knew I would eventually catch you coming or going."

"You are very clever," Leonardo congratulated him.

At last they drew close to the cottage. When he judged they were within earshot, Leonardo announced loudly, "This is the place, I swear it by the Blessed Virgin."

"Keep your voice down, fool," growled Rodrigo. "If the slave runs off, you will pay dearly."

Leonardo bowed like an incompetent servant. "My apologies, sir. I did not know that you cared so little for the Blessed Virgin."

"Be quiet about the Blessed Virgin!" the Spaniard grated.

"Forgive me, sir. How could I know you would take offence at the name of Our Lady?" He added on a louder note, "I did not know that you held the Blessed Virgin in contempt."

"Silence, you prattling fool—"

The next instant the cottage door flew open and the Brawler burst out like a bull crashing through a fence. "Who dishonours the name of the Blessed Virgin?" he demanded, his eyes aglow with righteous fury.

Rodrigo's lip curled. "Step aside, oaf. I have business here."

"The only business you have is with my fist, blasphemer!" the Brawler bellowed, brandishing a fist the size of a bucket.

As if by magic, a long-bladed dagger appeared in Rodrigo's hand. He made a lightning feint with it, too fast even for Leonardo's eye to follow.

Brawler cocked an eyebrow and laughed. "Do you plan to darn my breeches with that needle?"

"Buffoon! I will gut you like a pig if you do not move aside," Rodrigo warned.

A growl started up at the back of the Brawler's throat.

His brow buckled into deep furrows and his bushy eyebrows collided in the narrow space above his nose. His nostrils flared like a dragon's preparing to expel a blast of flame and his lips tightened into a ferocious grimace that exposed the great blocks of his teeth.

"Infidel!" he roared. "Heretic!"

Brandishing his granite fist, he charged.

Taken aback by this display of insane fearlessness, Rodrigo paused for a split second before striking.

Leonardo leapt and tried to grab the Spaniard's wrist, but, lithe as a snake, Rodrigo twisted loose, raking the steel point down Leonardo's sleeve. A thin, red line seared his arm like a streak of fire.

Even as Leonardo cried out, the Brawler's fist smashed into the Spaniard's cheek with a sound like a mallet smacking a side of beef. Rodrigo was knocked completely off his feet. His weapon went flying, casting off droplets of blood as it fell.

The Brawler stood over the senseless body and rubbed his head. "Who is this sinner?" he asked.

Before Leonardo could think of an adequate reply, Caterina ran up to him. She ushered him inside and made him sit down, clucking irritably over his wound, as though he had torn his jerkin in some boyish prank.

Fresina pushed aside her breakfast and leaned towards him. "What has happened? Did you hurt yourself."

Leonardo gritted his teeth against the pain. "No, I didn't hurt myself," he told her. "It was Rodrigo, Neroni's man."

Fresina put a hand to her mouth. "They have found us?"

"He was alone," Leonardo assured her. "I think his coming here was a gamble, but it almost paid off."

"Hush!" said Caterina. "Hold still while I tend this. Madalena, fetch fresh water from the stream. Gemma, get some linen." The two girls jumped to obey.

While Caterina washed and dressed the wound, the Brawler came in, dragging the unconscious Spaniard by the scruff of his doublet.

"Is he dead?" Fresina asked.

"No," the Brawler assured her heartily, "but he will not speak ill of the Blessed Virgin again."

The little boy, Maffeo, came scampering in waving his arms excitedly. "Mama! Papa! Another stranger is coming!"

Fresina turned on Leonardo. "I thought you said he was alone?"

"He was," Leonardo insisted. He tensed as a shadow appeared in the doorway. Then he relaxed.

"It's all right. It's my Uncle Francesco."

Francesco entered and bowed politely to both Caterina and the Brawler.

Caterina narrowed her eyes. "Francesco da Vinci," she said in a brittle voice. "I never thought to see you within these walls."

"Did Father send you?" Leonardo asked.

"No, he thinks you've gone back to Florence," said Francesco. "But I thought if you were really in trouble, you might come here." A proud smile lit his simple face. "Maybe this time I was smarter than Piero for a change."

"And why did *you* come?" Caterina asked him icily.

"To help, if I can," said Francesco with such obvious honesty that Caterina's expression immediately softened. Francesco looked down at Rodrigo. "Who is this?"

"A blasphemer," the Brawled announced.

"He came here to kill us," said Leonardo.

"What are you going to do with him?" Francesco asked.

The question silenced everyone except Fresina. "We should cut his heart out and feed it to the wolves," she declared. She made a stabbing motion with her hand as if to indicate that she was prepared to do the deed herself.

"We're in enough trouble already without committing murder," said Leonardo.

"Oh, so you will offer him a good meal and send him

back to the city to bring an army after us?" Fresina asked mockingly. "He is an enemy and he deserves no mercy from us."

"He is no danger now," said the Brawler. "If he wakes, I will hit him again."

"You can't stand over him all day, punching him every time he stirs," said Leonardo.

Caterina had been thinking in silence. "Leonardo, you did not reach the boat?" she asked.

"No, he ambushed me on my way there."

"Then we should tie this man up and gag him," said Caterina. "Place him in the boat, cover him up and set it adrift."

"Yes!" Leonardo agreed enthusiastically. "With any luck it will carry him all the way to Pisa before it runs aground."

"I've a wagon up the road a ways," Francesco offered. "We can take him in that."

While Francesco fetched his wagon, the Brawler trussed Rodrigo up so tightly with rope and leather straps Leonardo wondered if he would be able to breathe. A rag tied across his mouth completed his bondage.

At the sound of Francesco's return, the Brawler hefted the Spaniard on to one brawny shoulder. He carried

Rodrigo outside and dumped him into the wagon like a sack of turnips.

As the two men set off with their prisoner, the Brawler laughed and gave Francesco a friendly clap on the back that almost knocked the wind out of him.

Leonardo turned to his mother and Fresina. "I have to go back to Florence," he said.

"You are mad," said Fresina. "We should run as far away from the city as we can."

"If Neroni and his friends take over Florence, we will never be safe, no matter how far we run," said Leonardo.

Fresina hung her head dejectedly. "You are right."

"But how will you get there?" asked Caterina.

"I know where Rodrigo's horse is," said Leonardo. He smiled weakly. "I think it likes me."

Fresina stepped between Leonardo and the door. "If you are going back, then I must go to."

Leonardo shook his head vigorously. "It's dangerous enough just me going."

Caterina laid a gentle hand on the girl's shoulder. "You can stay here with us. I know a place we can hide you if anyone should come."

Fresina thrust out her lower lip defiantly. "Without me to watch him, he will just get in trouble," she declared.

"What if he falls down a well? Or is eaten by bears? Must I then stay hidden for ever?"

Leonardo looked hard at Fresina and for the first time believed he was seeing her as she truly was. Ever since the Torre Donati he had thought of himself as her rescuer. He had not stopped to think of the courage she had shown in striking down Neroni. And now she was ready to return to Florence with him, even though she knew only too well the awful fate that awaited her if she were caught. Of the two of them, he realised, she was the brave one.

"All right," he said, "you can come. I suppose I need someone to protect me from the bears."

Caterina took them both by the hand and drew them close. "I cannot see where this will all lead," she said, "but remember there will always be a place here – for either of you."

15

Cogs and Wheels

By the time Sandro answered the rapping at his window, Leonardo's knuckles were red from knocking. When he threw open the shutters, Sandro almost choked at the sight of his friend. Leonardo did not wait for a greeting but climbed nimbly inside and made his way to the nearest chair.

Fresina clambered in after him. She was dressed in a threadbare smock with a sackcloth scarf wrapped around her head. Sandro's eyes bulged as if a wildcat had just bounded into the room. "What are *you* doing here?"

"Waiting for you to let us in," the girl answered sharply.

She pulled off the scarf and shook her hair loose. "What took you so long?"

Sandro slammed the shutters on the stink of the canal and turned up the lantern. "I was finishing breakfast," he said, displaying the sweet pastry in his hand.

Fresina snatched the pastry from his fingers and wolfed it down hungrily. "We have not eaten for hours," she said, perching herself on the edge of Sandro's drawing table.

Sandro turned to gaze quizzically at Leonardo's garb: a simple peasant smock and a wide-brimmed straw hat that threw his face into shadow. "I can only imagine how you must be suffering in that outfit."

"It makes a good disguise," said Leonardo. "We sneaked through the gate in the middle of a band of farmers on their way to the market."

Sandro shook his head. "You're mad to come back. Do you know what will happen to you if you're caught?"

"We tried to run," said Leonardo, "but the Spaniard came after us."

"That one!" spat Fresina. "He is an evil spirit in the flesh of a man!"

Sandro raised his eyebrows. "Does she always talk this way?"

Fresina snorted and picked up a cup of water from the

table. She sniffed at it then drained it in one draught.

"I was planning on washing my brushes in that," Sandro objected lamely.

"What's been happening while I've been away?" Leonardo asked.

Sandro raised his hands in the air. "What hasn't been happening! The Constable's men are out looking for you and Luca Pitti has offered a reward to anyone who captures either one of you."

"What about Neroni?"

"He says this is typical of the lawlessness encouraged by having a sick man like Piero de' Medici ruling over Florence. I know it doesn't make sense, but that's politics."

"What does he say happened that day?"

"The story is all over the city, just as he reported it to the Constable. He claims that he was paying a call upon Lucrezia's father, Ser Paolo Donati, accompanied by his manservant Rodrigo. They were admitted by the chamberlain Tomasso who informed them that his master was away in Siena."

"Pah!" Fresina exclaimed. "He knew that when he came. Everyone knew."

Sandro ignored her and continued. "Neroni claims he sent Tomasso upstairs to fetch paper so he could leave a message for Signor Donati. There then came a cry and the sound of a struggle. Neroni and his man ran upstairs to see what was amiss. They entered the room to find the slave girl and a vicious-looking youth standing over Tomasso's bleeding body."

"Vicious-looking!" Leonardo exclaimed.

"I'm only telling you what I heard," said Sandro. "The two criminals, he says, barged past them and escaped into the street. When Lucrezia Donati returned home she discovered that several items of jewellery had been stolen, presumably by the runaway slave girl and her accomplice."

Leonardo noticed that Sandro was rubbing his injured arm as he spoke. "How's your wrist?" he asked.

"A lot better," Sandro said, brightening. "I think those old remedies of my mother's really work. I only wish they didn't stink so much."

"What's happened to the portrait?"

"It was so badly damaged in the struggle you had with Neroni and his man, I'll have to start again from scratch. Fortunately that means Lorenzo no longer expects it in a couple of days time. I'll soon be recovered enough to do it all myself."

"What about your friends the Medici?" Leonardo

asked. "Don't they understand that Tomasso's murder is part of a plot against them?"

"Piero de' Medici, Il Gottoso, is stricken with his usual gout and has retired to his villa in the country. Lorenzo is here in the city, but he has no basis to act against Neroni. Neroni and his puppet Luca Pitti grow bolder by the day. They've gathered so many men at Pitti's palace they've as good as taken over the Oltrarno. There's even a rumour the Duke of Ferrara is on his way with an army to support them."

They were suddenly silenced by the slap of sandals on the floor outside the room. Then the door swung open.

Instinctively, Leonardo dived behind a table. Fresina tried to dodge into hiding, but bumped into Sandro who was trying to block her from sight. The girl fell into his arms and that was how Sandro's mother found them as she stepped into the room with a fresh plate of sweet pastries in her hand.

Red-faced, Sandro pushed Fresina away and made a flustered attempt to straighten his tunic. There was a mischievous glint in the old woman's eye. "I brought you some pastries to keep you going until lunch. I didn't know you had company."

"Company?" Sandro squeaked. "No, no, she's… she's… a model."

"A model?"

"Yes, her name is… Proserpina."

"I didn't see her come in."

"She came in… er… she came…" Sandro stammered helplessly.

"I came in through the window," Fresina interjected. "I could not find the front door."

His mother squinted at Fresina and tutted. "She's very thin for a model. She should eat more."

"That is true," Fresina agreed, helping herself to the plate of pastries and settling down in the corner to devour them.

Sandro ushered his mother out and collapsed against the door. Leonardo emerged from hiding and wiped the sweat from his brow.

"He is a very poor liar," Fresina commented through a mouthful of pastry.

"Not all of us are born to it," said Leonardo.

"And what is that stupid name, Prosperina?" Fresina snorted.

"ProsERpina," Sandro corrected her. "A Roman goddess of the Netherworld. It seemed appropriate somehow."

"Look, Sandro," Leonardo interrupted, "the only chance I have of getting out of this is to expose whatever plot Neroni and his gang are brewing, and this is the only crack I have at it." He pulled out the drawing and spread it out before him.

"That again?" groaned Sandro. "I know you can't resist trying to solve a puzzle, but there are serious matters at stake here."

"It's more than a puzzle," Leonardo insisted. "Tell me what you know about Silvestro."

"Well, it's a sad story," Sandro recalled. "Silvestro was a pupil of the famous artist Donatello and showed great promise from an early age. Until a couple of years ago he had a thriving business, a large shop and more than a dozen apprentices. But then he fell into bad company, drinking and gambling. It was about that time his design for the tomb of Cosimo de' Medici was rejected. From then on Silvestro's decline became even more extreme."

"Yes, it all makes sense," mused Leonardo. "He will do anything now for enough money to re-establish his career, and added to that, he has a grudge against the Medici."

"That still doesn't tell us what this drawing of yours is supposed to be," said Sandro.

Fresina ducked around Sandro's shoulder and peered at the drawing. "It is a spell," she said, chewing on a pastry. "I have seen shamans in Circassia draw patterns like this in the earth to cast curses upon their enemies."

Sandro took an uneasy step away from her. "Well, I'm no more an engineer than you are," he said to Leonardo, "and I can't tell what it's supposed to be. Do you think it's a siege engine?"

"No, the dimensions are written here," said Leonardo. He paused to wipe away the crumbs that had fallen on to the paper from Fresina's pastry. "It would be no bigger than that chair over there."

"Then I don't see what sort of threat it could be," said Sandro. "Are you sure you haven't left something out?"

Leonardo tugged at his hair and cast his mind back. He remembered now that Silvestro had flipped the drawing over. And there were some scribbles on the back. "Yes," he said, "there was more. Not part of the diagram, but some sort of writing on the back of the sheet."

He picked up a piece of charcoal and carefully drew in a set of symbols in the top left-hand corner of the paper. Sandro leaned close and peered at them.

The first was a circle with an arrow projecting out of it to the left. Next, a cross with a hook attached to the left arm. And finally another circle with a cross hanging from the bottom of it.

"And what's this you're adding?" Sandro asked as Leonardo sketched in some further details.

"Well, there were lines radiating downward from the symbols towards a plain circle a few inches below," said Leonardo. "Then more circles and lines."

"It looks like angles are being measured," Sandro suggested.

"But what about the signs?" said Leonardo. "I've never seen anything like them. Is it some foreign script?"

Sandro shook his head thoughtfully. "No," he said, "but they are familiar. Once my master Fra Lippi took me to the house of the astronomer Toscanelli. He used signs like these in his charts to represent stars or planets or some such thing."

Fresina wrinkled her face. "Planets?"

"Stars that don't keep to a fixed position but move around the sky," Sandro explained.

"Ah, we know them in Circassia," said Fresina. "They are the daughters of Tleps, the fire god. You see? I told you there was sorcery in this."

"Stars? Planets?" Leonardo banged his fist down on the drawing in frustration. "But that makes no sense at all!" He chewed his lip for a moment. "There's only one thing to do," he decided. "We have to go and see this astronomer, Toscanelli. Maybe he can tell us how the stars can be made into a weapon."

"I shall make him talk," said Fresina.

"No, you're going to stay here," Leonardo told her firmly.

"You leave me here?" the girl protested.

"They're looking for the two of us. There's more chance we'll be recognised if we go together. If we're caught, you know what will happen."

"Very well, I shall stay," Fresina agreed grudgingly. "But only if Sandro's mother brings more pastries."

16

The Door to the Universe

They had no trouble finding Toscanelli's house. It reared up above the surrounding rooftops like a stony finger pointed emphatically at the heavens.

Sandro had borrowed a splendid red coat from one of his brothers and over this he wore a jewelled amulet of his mother's. "Remember to let me do all the talking," he warned. "This is a very distinguished scholar who has no time for riff-raff. I will take on the role of a fine gentleman, and you will be my servant."

"Your servant?"

"Dressed like that, what else could you possibly be?"

Sandro yanked on the bell pull. After a few moments an elderly woman opened the door the merest crack.

"Well?" she demanded suspiciously.

"I am here to see the noble Maestro Paolo da Pozzo Toscanelli," Sandro announced grandly. He was being so grand he did not even look at the woman when he spoke to her.

"Is he expecting you?" the woman asked. She did not sound impressed.

"In a manner of speaking," Sandro answered – not so convincingly, in Leonardo's view. "The wise man expects everything in advance, no matter how unexpected it may be."

"He knows you, does he?" the woman inquired.

"Are you casting doubt upon the breadth of his knowledge?" Sandro countered. "How could he not know me?"

The woman frowned and mumbled to herself. "I suppose you had better come in," she conceded. "Perhaps the master will know what you're talking about."

She opened the door, admitting them to a reception hall from which a stairway ascended to the upper reaches of the house. "Wait here while I inform the master of your arrival," she said. "By the way, who are you?"

"Tell him the noted artist Alessandro di Mariano Filipepi is here on a matter of great importance," Sandro instructed her.

Leonardo groaned inwardly. He had never heard Sandro use his proper name before and it sounded very pompous.

The woman started stiffly up the stairway. As soon as she was out of sight, Leonardo rounded on his friend. "Did you really have to talk such rubbish?"

"It got us in here, didn't it?" Sandro retorted. "Besides, you need to remember that I am the master here. I'll thank you to show me some respect."

A long time dragged by before the servant reappeared and beckoned them to follow her upstairs. She took them to an upper room and left them there. It was a library, the walls lined with books and scrolls. On a desk there were sheets of parchment covered with rows of figures. Beside them lay an assortment of mathematical instruments, interlocking wheels and elaborate brass dials.

"You see, we've come to the right place," Sandro observed with satisfaction. "This is a man of knowledge. Look, he has the works of Aristotle, Strabo, Ptolemy."

"Yes, I'm sure they're all good friends of his," said Leonardo distractedly.

A door opened and a tall, elderly man entered the room. Below his wide brow a long, hooked nose overshadowed his rounded lips. From his slight chin a narrow beard curled down to his chest like a silver ribbon. He was dressed in colourful eastern robes and a turban that made him look more like a wizard than a scholar.

The two visitors bowed but Toscanelli did not seem interested in their display of good manners. He peered at Sandro as though he were a rare species of beetle.

"I didn't recognise the name you gave, but I'm sure I recognise you," he said.

"I was here once before with Fra Filippo Lippi," said Sandro.

A merry twinkle appeared in Toscanelli's sharp eyes. "Lippi, that rogue," he beamed. "Where is he? Chasing the girls as usual, I suppose."

Sandro cleared his throat. "I believe he is engaged on an altarpiece."

Toscanelli let out a bark of laughter then peered at Sandro again. "Lippi had a different name for you. Botticelli he said your name was – the Little Barrel."

"A nickname I have acquired through my brother," said Sandro. "It seems to have stuck with me."

"And this is...?" The astronomer waved at Leonardo.

"His cousin," Leonardo put in quickly before Sandro could speak.

Sandro winced as though someone had stepped on his toe. "Yes, my cousin," he agreed reluctantly. "A simple country lad I have taken under my wing. I'm doing my best to broaden his mind."

"Then you've come to the right place," Toscanelli chortled. "So what do you think of my library, young man?"

"I haven't read many books," Leonardo replied uneasily.

"That's good!" Toscanelli declared. "That means your mind is your own. My work is devoted to proving most of them wrong anyway," he added with a chuckle. "But perhaps I can impress you with something else."

Beckoning them to follow, he started up the spiral staircase in the corner of the room. This led to a plain door, where the astronomer halted. "Do you know what I keep in this room?" he asked, with an impish glint in his eye.

"More books?" Sandro offered.

Toscanelli laughed.

"Treasure?" said Leonardo.

Toscanelli laughed even louder and patted Leonardo on the shoulder. "You at least are closer to the truth than your cousin. In here I keep the whole *Universe*." He accompanied this statement with a grandiose sweep of his arm that set his baggy sleeve flapping in Leonardo's face. Then he flung open the door and led his visitors inside.

A round wooden table occupied the centre of the room and spread out across it was a sheet of fine goatskin parchment. On this was painted a map of the world, from the westernmost tip of Spain to the fabled empire of Cathay, from the sun-scorched deserts of Libya to the frozen island of Thule in the furthest north.

Snaky blue rivers spread like veins across the lands where painted towers, trees and weird beasts illustrated the wonders of each country. Surrounding the sweeping mass of the continents was the vast ocean, its gleaming blue surface dotted with tiny islands and its edges churned to a froth by the writhing coils of the monstrous serpents that were believed to lurk out there.

The curving walls of the room were covered with elaborate charts that marked out the entire night sky. Delicately traced over the patterns of the stars were beautiful pictures of the constellations: a hunter with his hounds, a pair of twins, a scorpion, a bull and all the other inhabitants of the heavens. The star maps spread up the walls and over the vaulted ceiling. From the centre of the vault hung a silver lantern that illuminated the world below like a miniature moon.

Leonardo and Sandro stared in wonder, their eyes drifting from the colourful outlines of the earth to the circuit of the skies that encircled them on every side.

Seeing their expressions, Toscanelli beamed proudly and waved a hand over the map. "Here, you see, I am making a grid across the earth. Once I have completed my measurements, I intend to chart a course that will take a ship across the western sea, around the globe of the world to India and Cathay. And who knows what mysterious islands might be discovered along the way, what strange tribes and wondrous beasts!"

He pointed to some lines on his sky charts. "Here I have recorded the paths of comets across the quarters of the firmament. How many nights I have gone without sleep measuring their progress! But how much I have learned as a result! Contrary to Aristotle, I have proved that the comets move beyond the orbit of the moon and that they follow regular courses, just as the planets do."

"The planets!" Sandro exclaimed, as though he had just woken from a dream. "That's why we're here."

Toscanelli glared down his nose. "If you have come here for a horoscope, I suggest you go now. I leave those matters to quacks and deceivers."

"That's not what he means," said Leonardo. He reached into his tunic and pulled out the drawing. He had carefully folded the paper so that only the part showing the mysterious symbols was exposed. "We came across this sketch," he said, "but we don't know what to make of it."

"We were hoping you could shed some light," Sandro added.

"You intrigue me," Toscanelli said. "Let me see."

Leonardo handed over the paper. The astronomer took out a pair of spectacles and balanced them on his nose. Then he peered at the drawing and tilted his head curiously to one side, running a finger over it and making a low whistling noise between his teeth.

"Do you understand it?" Leonardo asked.

"Of course I understand it," Toscanelli replied distractedly. "This symbol on the left – the circle with the arrow – that represents the planet Mars. The next one – the hooked cross – is Jupiter. And the third – the circle with the cross – signifies Venus, the morning star."

"And the lines coming from them, those are the movements of the planets?" Sandro inquired.

"Don't be absurd," said Toscanelli. "The Greek astronomer Ptolemy demonstrated centuries ago that the planets move in circles around the earth, not in straight lines. There's some sort of relationship of lines and angles marked out here, but it has nothing to do with planetary orbits."

"Then we've solved nothing," Leonardo sighed.

"Not necessarily," said Toscanelli. With a flick of his wrist he threw open the entire sheet and laid it on his desk where he smoothed out the creases with his long bony fingers.

Leonardo started. He had not intended to entrust the astronomer with the plan of the machine, and moved to snatch it away, but Sandro signalled him to stay back.

Toscanelli ran a finger over the drawing, sucking on his teeth as he examined the details. "What is this intended to be?" he asked.

"I'm not sure," said Leonardo. "But it's very important that we learn what it does."

"Oh, I can answer that question easily," said Toscanelli. "It doesn't do anything at all."

17

The Secret of the Egg

Leonardo stormed off down the street, one hand clapped hard to his hat, his face set in a glowering rage.

"I don't see why you're taking this so badly," Sandro panted as he struggled to keep up.

"It can't be true," Leonardo said vehemently. "It must work."

"You heard what Toscanelli said," Sandro told him. "The parts don't connect up. If you built this machine, it would do nothing at all."

"He's wrong," Leonardo asserted stubbornly. "The machine must work."

"Oh, so the great Toscanelli, the most brilliant man in Florence, is wrong," said Sandro, "and you, Leonardo da Vinci, the apprentice, the boy from the country, you are right?"

"Yes," said Leonardo firmly. "I must be right, otherwise nothing makes sense."

They stepped aside and pressed themselves against the nearest wall to avoid a flock of sheep that was being driven down the street towards the market. Once the sheep had passed they made their way to the Piazza del Duomo, the square that spread out before the entrance to the cathedral. The cathedral was always referred to as the Duomo, the House of God.

"It may be that you simply made a mistake in your copy of the drawing," said Sandro.

"I didn't make a mistake," Leonardo insisted testily. "It's all up here, exactly as I saw it." He tapped himself on the head.

"In that case I give up," Sandro declared, throwing his hands in the air. "There's no way to make sense of this."

"You can give up if you like," said Leonardo, "but I will not."

Above their heads the vast dome of the cathedral dominated the city's skyline. It was regarded by all

Florentines as one of the wonders of the world.

Leonardo pointed up at the dome. "Maestro Andrea told me that when the engineer Filippo Brunelleschi first proposed building this dome, the members of the Signoria said it was impossible, that anything so large would collapse under its own weight."

"It's not the same thing," said Sandro.

"Yes, it is," said Leonardo. "Filippo said that any man who could balance an egg on its end could build the dome."

"I know the story," said Sandro. "When the councillors said it was impossible to make an egg stand on its end, Filippo took an egg and cracked it on the bottom to make it stay upright."

"Exactly. Sometimes, all that we need to achieve the impossible is one simple idea."

As they rounded the corner into the cathedral square, a parade of men appeared, marching under an array of banners, most of which were decorated with the picture of a leopard.

"What's this?" asked Leonardo. "A religious procession?"

Sandro grabbed him and pulled him into the shadow of an overhanging balcony. "It's only religious if you share Luca Pitti's high opinion of himself," he said. "That leopard is his family crest."

He pointed to a white-haired figure on a splendid horse who was riding in the centre of the marching column. He was dressed in robes of silk and gold and he waved airily to the crowd as he passed. Here and there some sporadic cheers broke out and cries of, "The Hill! The Hill! Hail to Luca Pitti!"

The horseman looked as if he were bored by all the attention, but was forcing himself to acknowledge the applause out of the sheer generosity of his heart.

Leonardo stared at the pompous figure. "That's Luca Pitti?"

"Yes," said Sandro. "The Saviour of Florence, he would have us believe."

"What is he saving us from?"

Sandro shrugged. "You tell me. I'll wager that half the people cheering him are doing so because they've been paid in advance to put on a show."

"He doesn't look very dangerous," Leonardo observed.

"He isn't, but Neroni is – and he may not be far behind," said Sandro. "Pull your hat down lower. Someone might see your face."

"I'm not as famous as you seem to think," said Leonardo. "I've only been in Florence a few months and hardly anybody knows me."

"We only have to run into *one* of them for us to end up in jail," said Sandro.

As soon as the parade had passed, Leonardo noticed a young man climbing up the steps of the Duomo. He tugged on his friend's sleeve and pointed. "Look, it's Lorenzo de' Medici."

Sandro stared as the figure disappeared behind the heavy brass doors of the cathedral. "Are you sure?"

"Even from this distance it's hard to mistake him," said Leonardo. "I need to go and talk to him."

"Are you insane? What makes you think he won't turn you over to the Constable?"

"For one thing, he's never seen me before," said Leonardo, "so he won't recognise me. For another, the Medici may be the only allies I have against Neroni."

Sandro rubbed his brow in agitation. "All right. I suppose I'd better come with you."

"No. If he does realise who I am, then you'd be incriminated too. You go home and take care of Fresina."

"Take care of her?" Sandro shuddered. "You know, I'm not so sure she hasn't killed anybody."

"It's the entire Botticelli family against one girl," said Leonardo. "I think you'll manage."

He hurried across the square, trying not to draw attention to himself. He slipped through the doorway, leaving the noise and heat of the square for the vast, cool interior of the Duomo. Leonardo removed his hat as a sign of respect and tucked it under his arm.

A heavy tang of incense hung in the air. A long floor of polished marble stretched down to the altar where a priest was intoning the Latin words of the mass over a crowd of worshippers. Here and there people stood before the statues of saints, murmuring their private prayers.

Leonardo looked around and quickly spotted the bulbous nose and jutting jaw of Lorenzo de' Medici looming out of the shadow of a pillar, like the leering face of a gargoyle. Lorenzo was peering about as if he was expecting to see someone. Leonardo stepped closer and coughed to draw attention to himself.

"Signor Lorenzo?"

An old woman running prayer beads through her fingers stopped and glared at the noise. Leonardo immediately lowered his head and his voice.

Lorenzo turned and took him in at a glance. "Yes?"

"I'm sorry to interrupt you," said Leonardo, "but I have some important information you should know."

"I'm not buying information today," said Lorenzo, waving him away.

"But it is most urgent," Leonardo insisted.

In the background he heard the priest utter the final blessing to dismiss the worshippers. People rose from their seats and began filing towards the door.

"Many things are urgent," said Lorenzo off-handedly. "I'm afraid they will have to form an orderly line and wait their turn."

He was scanning the faces of the congregation as they passed.

Leonardo held his ground. "Do you know the artist Silvestro?"

Lorenzo glanced round and quirked a curious eyebrow. "He used to do some work for my family. I remember when I was a boy he designed a mechanical dragon for the annual procession on the feast day of John the Baptist. When it opened its jaws smoke and fire belched out of its mouth. It was the talk of Florence for months."

"Well, he's been working on something else," said Leonardo, "made from bronze, I suspect. This is a copy I made of the plans I saw in his workshop." He took out the drawing and began to unfold it.

"What has this to do with me?" Lorenzo inquired.

Leonardo was irked at not being taken seriously. "It was your enemy Neroni who commissioned this device," he said sharply.

Lorenzo immediately stiffened. "Neroni? Do you know this for sure?"

"I saw his henchman, Rodrigo, at Silvestro's workshop. He was impatient for the work to be finished. Can't you see the danger you're in?"

"Why should I be in any danger because of a work of art?" Lorenzo asked.

"Because of your family," said Leonardo. "Because your father is the ruler of Florence."

"My father is a simple businessman," Lorenzo asserted flatly.

"That may be, but Neroni and Pitti are plotting to do away with both of you," said Leonardo, "and this is part of it." He shook the drawing under Lorenzo's nose.

"Very well then," Lorenzo said. "Tell me what it is."

Leonardo bit his lip and silently cursed his ignorance. "I don't know yet."

Lorenzo's eyes narrowed sceptically. "You're not making much of a case."

Suddenly, his manner changed and Leonardo saw Lucrezia approaching from the direction of the altar. He realised that this was who Lorenzo had come to meet.

The girl's face was aglow like sunlight. "Lorenzo, I was afraid you hadn't come," she chided playfully. Then she saw Leonardo and her almond eyes flared in shock. "Leonardo da Vinci!"

"Da Vinci?" Lorenzo exclaimed. "Is this the boy who is wanted for murder?"

Lucrezia nodded mutely.

Leonardo started to back away, but Lorenzo seized him by the front of his smock. His grip was surprisingly strong. "Did you follow me here just to run away?" he demanded. There was a steely challenge in his voice.

"I came to give you a warning."

"Yes, and a pretty lot of nonsense it was too. What is this game you're playing?"

Leonardo was tongue-tied, too confused to answer Lorenzo's suspicions. Meeting the young Medici face to face was a very different thing to observing him from hiding. There was an energy about him that was both commanding and intimidating.

"Where is Fresina?" Lucrezia asked with genuine concern.

"She is safe," said Leonardo. "I swear to you, she's no killer and neither am I."

"Oh no?" said Lorenzo. "There is a man dead."

"It was Neroni's henchman, the Spaniard, who did that. And Neroni was there too."

Lorenzo's jaw hardened. "Be careful of your words, Leonardo da Vinci. Do you know what will happen if you repeat that charge openly?"

They suddenly noticed that one of the priests had stopped in his tracks to stare at them. Lorenzo released Leonardo and waved to the priest, his face lighting up in an easy smile.

"If you try to escape," he murmured aside to Leonardo, "I'll alert the entire cathedral to who you are. Now follow me."

He took Lucrezia gently by the elbow and guided her into a nearby alcove that was lit by a row of white candles. Leonardo followed.

"Lorenzo, it is too fantastic," said Lucrezia. "Why would anyone want to kill Tomasso?"

"He was spying for Neroni," Leonardo explained, "keeping a watch on the two of you and reporting your movements."

"How do you know all this?" Lorenzo asked curtly.

"Fresina heard most of it," Leonardo replied. "That's why they tried to kill her too. We harmed no one. We only ran away to save our own lives."

"That is for the Constable to decide," said Lorenzo. "I hope you have a better story for him than the one you've told me."

"If I'm locked up," Leonardo protested, "there will be no one to find out the truth about this." He shook the paper at Lorenzo.

"What is that?" Lucrezia asked.

"Some drawing," Lorenzo replied dismissively. "It would be a comic tale if the matter were not so serious."

"I need to go to Silvestro's workshop," said Leonardo. "The device may still be there. Or would you rather see Luca Pitti become ruler of Florence?"

Lucrezia pressed close to Lorenzo as if they were suddenly in the presence of a great unseen danger. "I cannot believe Luca Pitti is involved in this. He is a friend of my father."

Lorenzo frowned darkly at Leonardo. "I cannot be party to this insanity. My father has enough troubles already without my adding to them. I will escort you to the Constable and hand you over to him. After that, the court will decide your fate."

"You've already said no one will believe me," said Leonardo. "Aren't you just sentencing me to death?"

"And what would you have me do? Take your word and try to have Neroni arrested? Or should I set you free and make a criminal of myself?"

The force of Lorenzo's challenge left Leonardo floundering for an answer. He returned the drawing to its place under his tunic, still smarting at how easily Lorenzo had dismissed it.

"A cathedral is an unsuitable place to discuss such things," said Lorenzo. "Come and we will set the matter before the Constable."

He took Lucrezia's arm and started for the door. Leonardo realised how hard it was to refuse the young Medici once his mind was made up and he followed them dejectedly. He put his hat back on as he emerged into the sunlight, then pulled up sharply to avoid bumping into Lorenzo and Lucrezia who had come to an abrupt halt.

There, at the bottom of the cathedral steps, was Neroni, waiting for them like a cat in front of a mousehole.

18

Beneath the Dome

Leonardo hurriedly ducked his head, hiding his features beneath the wide brim of his hat. Neroni rested one hand on the hilt of his sword and waved the other in a flowery salute to Lorenzo.

Lorenzo remained calm and even smiled pleasantly. “Signor Neroni, I am afraid you are too late for mass.”

“That is not why I’m here,” said Neroni. “I bring a message for the lovely Lucrezia Donati.”

With a flourish of his hand, he bowed low in Lucrezia’s direction. Lucrezia tilted her head in acknowledgement, but turned her face away.

Lorenzo's wiry shoulders stiffened as at the prick of a dagger. "You're putting yourself to some trouble to deliver it. Couldn't it have been left at the Torre Donati?"

"Ah, but that is the point of the message," said Neroni. "After the distressing incident at her home the other day and with so much unrest in the city, it seems advisable that the lady should be taken to a place of safety." His voice was oily with concern. "Therefore, our most prominent citizen, the noble Luca Pitti, has opened his home to her and insists that she accept his protection until her father returns from Siena."

He beckoned to a coach that was standing close by with its door open. It was painted with the same leopard symbol Leonardo had seen in Luca Pitti's procession. Two attendants waited there to help Lucrezia aboard.

Leonardo glanced over at Lucrezia and saw her flash a brilliant smile. "Luca Pitti is generous, as always," she said, "but I really am in no danger." Her voice was light and carefree, as if they were chatting pleasantly at a dinner party.

"Luca Pitti was most insistent," said Neroni.

He snapped his fingers. Four men who had been loitering in the background promptly formed a semi-circle behind him, sweeping back their cloaks to reveal the swords at their sides. Leonardo was painfully aware that he and Lorenzo had no weapons of their own.

Seemingly undaunted, Lorenzo took a firm pace forward, placing himself between Lucrezia and Neroni. "The lady is under *my* protection," he stated forcefully.

"I'm afraid that gives me little confidence," said Neroni, advancing up the steps. "Especially in view of the company you keep."

Darting past Lorenzo, he whipped the straw hat from Leonardo's head. "This boy is a wanted murderer," he said, tossing the hat away.

The four armed men closed in and Lorenzo eyed them warily.

"Do not resist, Lorenzo," said Neroni with a smirk. "You are unarmed after all."

"You will not find me so again," said Lorenzo. "I promise you that."

Lucrezia took a deep breath. "There is no need for trouble here, Signor Neroni," she said. "I am happy to accept the hospitality of the noble Luca Pitti, since his heart is set on doing me this service."

Leonardo heard the faintest tremor in her voice, and knew that it was Lorenzo she feared for, not herself. As she started towards the carriage, Lorenzo tried to follow, but

Lucrezia turned and placed a hand on his breast to stop him.

"No, Lorenzo, let's not risk any trouble here. Luca Pitti will not allow me to come to harm."

"The lady is correct," Neroni agreed. "Surely you do not doubt the integrity of our leading citizen."

"It is not *his* integrity I doubt," Lorenzo answered in a strained voice. His eyes smouldered helplessly as he watched Lucrezia get into the carriage. As she was driven off, she looked back and touched a finger to her lips.

Neroni shook his head disapprovingly and gestured towards Leonardo. "This casts you in a very bad light, Lorenzo, consorting with wanted criminals."

"That has yet to be proved," said Lorenzo.

"There is proof enough," Neroni snapped, waving his men forward. "I will take this boy to a place where he will pay for his crimes."

Leonardo swallowed. "If I go with them, I won't live to stand trial," he told Lorenzo.

Lorenzo fixed Leonardo with a probing stare, like a man trying to read the faded ink of an old manuscript. Abruptly, he turned back to Neroni. "You can leave him in my custody," he said. "I will vouch for his good behaviour."

Neroni raised a hand to halt his men. He leaned close to

Lorenzo and addressed him in a hushed tone. "I advise you strongly to co-operate with me. Your father is a sick man. If his health should give out or some other misfortune befall him, your position would be very perilous indeed."

"I never indulge in speculation," Lorenzo retorted.

"This is more than idle speculation," Neroni continued. "You know that some would press you to step into Piero's shoes, to guide the business of Florence as he has done. Such a course might put you and those you care about in considerable danger. Would it not be better if you took your inheritance and slipped away into voluntary exile in some quiet seaside town? Who knows? After a while, the lovely Lucrezia could join you there, once all this trouble is past."

Leonardo saw the muscles in Lorenzo's jaw twitch as he assessed his position. Finally, the young Medici fixed Neroni with an iron stare. "You have misjudged me if you think you can turn me into another of your puppets," he said.

Neroni sneered and fingered the hilt of his sword. "Think again, if not for your own sake, for that of your sweetheart."

"I have thought long enough," said Lorenzo.

Without warning he shoved Neroni with both hands and sent him toppling backwards down the steps. His men tumbled over themselves trying to break his fall and the five of them ended up in a tangle of limbs and cloaks at the foot of the steps.

"Inside!" Lorenzo snapped, darting back into the cathedral.

Leonardo shot after him. "So you believe me?" he asked.

"If you're lying, you're doing a better job of it than Neroni is," Lorenzo replied.

He cast a swift look around. Their sudden entrance had drawn startled looks from the few people inside the Duomo, but no one made a move to stop them.

Leonardo glanced back through the open door. Neroni and his men had clambered to their feet and were starting up the steps. "Neroni's coming after us!" he exclaimed.

"I have nothing left to say to that gentleman," said Lorenzo.

Together, they dashed down the centre of the cathedral. A troop of black-clad nuns jumped aside to avoid them as they raced towards the altar.

"I suppose you have a plan?" Leonardo gasped.

"Not yet," said Lorenzo. "I'm hoping something will turn up."

He vaulted over the altar rail and Leonardo leapt after

him. Over his shoulder he glimpsed Neroni's men drawing their swords as they pursued.

Up ahead the priest was just coming out of the sacristy, having hung up his robes after mass. Lorenzo barged past the astonished cleric and into the room, Leonardo tumbling in behind him.

Lorenzo slammed the door shut and hauled over a table to prop against it. Together, they added some chairs and a cabinet to the barricade. Then they looked around them. Priestly robes hung along the walls and the various instruments of the mass – candles, bowls and chalices – were laid out on the shelves. But there was no other door, only a small wooden stair in the far corner.

"Where does that go?" Leonardo wondered.

"Up to the choir loft," said Lorenzo. "A dead end."

"This is a cathedral," said Leonardo. "Can't we claim sanctuary from the bishop? The church is supposed to help those who throw themselves on her mercy."

"Not in this case, I'm afraid," said Lorenzo. "The bishop is Neroni's brother."

Leonardo's heart plummeted. The next moment the door shuddered at a violent blow from outside.

Neroni's voice resounded through the church. "Smash it in!"

"We have to go up," said Lorenzo. "At least we can defend ourselves better at the top of the stairs."

Leonardo did his best to visualise the interior of the cathedral outside the sacristy door. A plan had occurred to him. "Up it is," he agreed, "but grab some of those priests' robes on the way."

He snatched a set of green vestments from the wall and took off up the stairs.

"It's a little late to adopt a disguise," said Lorenzo, but he grabbed a set of robes anyway.

They scrambled up into the gallery then crouched low out of sight. Below, the thunder of fists on wood continued.

"The way they're pounding at that door, I doubt they'll hear us up here," said Lorenzo. "With any luck, they'll assume we're propping up our barricade."

Leonardo inched forward and peered over the railing. Above his head, the vast, empty curve of the dome swelled like a blank sky. Below, he could see the long marble floor stretching out towards the bronze door that led to safety. It was at least a twenty-foot drop. Hidden from view by the overhang of the gallery, Neroni's men continued their assault on the sacristy door. Leonardo couldn't imagine that it would hold out much longer.

He separated out the robes he had brought and started tying them together.

"Your plan is that we should climb down," Lorenzo said approvingly.

"Something like that," Leonardo grunted.

He added Lorenzo's robes to the makeshift lifeline. A part of his mind winced at having to crush and twist such fine fabrics. Lorenzo helped him secure the colourful rope to the gallery railing.

Praying that the knots would hold, Leonardo swung himself on to the rail and took a tight grip on the line. As Lorenzo made ready to follow, the sacristy door gave way with a loud crash.

"Quick! Up the stairs!" they heard Neroni bellow.

"Grab hold and jump for it!" Leonardo cried as heavy footsteps pounded up the wooden steps.

Gripping the bulky rope, they launched themselves off the rail and plunged towards the marble floor below. The line snapped taut. For an instant, their legs flailed in midair. Then the hastily tied knots broke loose.

They hit the floor with a thud, the loose vestments billowing down on top of them. Lorenzo jumped up first and pulled Leonardo to his feet.

They made a desperate dash down the length of the

cathedral. Behind them, Leonardo could hear Neroni raging at his men. By the time their pursuers had come clattering back down the stairway, the fugitives were outside. As they rushed down the steps, Leonardo bent to retrieve his hat which still lay where Neroni had thrown it. Shoving it back on his head, he raced across the square after Lorenzo. Diving into the shelter of a narrow alley, they stopped to take a breath.

"I must go straight to my father and mobilise our followers," said Lorenzo. "Come with me and tell him all you have told me."

Leonardo shook his head. "Everything that has happened is part of some scheme I can't quite see yet. But the key to it all is the machine. The only place I can find the answer is in Silvestro's workshop."

Lorenzo conceded the point with a wave of his hand. "Go then. I cannot waste time arguing while Lucrezia is in Neroni's hands."

Leonardo paused an instant. "Whatever happens," he said, "please see to it that Fresina is safe. She is being cared for by my friend, Sandro Botticelli."

"Of course," said Lorenzo. "Good luck to you."

He turned and hurried off to the north of the city. Leonardo headed in the other direction, towards the Oltrarno, towards the place where the mystery had begun.

19

Discovery and Danger

The noon bell was tolling in the tower of Santo Spirito and Leonardo could hear the congregation chanting their midday prayers inside. He averted his face as a troop of stonemasons marched past, heading for the Pitti Palace.

Retracing his step through the narrow streets that surrounded the church, he found himself once more outside Silvestro's dilapidated workshop. The sky was overcast and the air was heavy with impending thunder, which made the building look even more dreary than it had before.

The front door was closed, so he crawled beneath the

window and took a cautious peek over the ledge. The workshop was empty. He stood up and glanced around to make sure no one was passing, then slipped a leg over the ledge and climbed inside.

Tools had been abandoned willy-nilly, powder and paint lay carelessly uncovered, and scraps of paper and splinters of wood littered the dirty floor. On one of the worktables was a half-eaten loaf of bread, some crumbs of cheese and a pair of cups containing the dregs of cheap wine. Leonardo ran his finger around the rim of one of them and discovered it was still moist. Someone had been here this morning and there was no telling when they would return. He would have to make his search a quick one.

Leonardo cautiously approached Silvestro's private chamber and listened at the door. Hearing no sound, he stepped inside and found it empty. He sniffed the air, suddenly aware of a strange, unfamiliar odour. Unable to identify it, he dismissed it from his mind and made for the desk.

A brisk search of Silvestro's papers turned up nothing but overdue bills and half-finished sketches of human figures. There was no trace of the diagram he had seen before.

At the back of the room was a hanging decorated with a

picture of Vulcan, the blacksmith of the Roman pantheon. Leonardo pulled it aside to reveal an archway leading to the forge room. The floor was coated in a layer of soot and ash marked with so many footprints Leonardo wasn't afraid to add his own.

He crossed over to the furnace and laid a hand on it. It was completely cold. He looked around and saw some fragments of clay, the remains of moulds that had been deliberately smashed. Then, in one corner, he spotted something that made him catch his breath.

It was a chest, fastened with a padlock, and it was exactly the right size to hold the object he had come in search of. Leonardo pressed his palms down on the lid, as if by doing so he could sense what was inside. Surely it could be only one thing – Silvestro's machine.

He looked around for something to break the lock with and saw a long-handled shovel used for loading coal into a furnace. He grabbed it and stood over the chest.

Taking careful aim, he lifted the shovel above his head and swung. The iron blade slammed into the padlock, tossing off sparks. Leonardo struck again and again, until he was perspiring from the effort. Then he gave one last, almighty blow and the padlock broke, dropping to the floor with a clank.

Setting the shovel aside, Leonardo unfastened the front of his smock and flapped it to cool himself off. He reached for the chest and realised his hand was trembling. The prospect of finally uncovering the secret was so exciting he could hardly bring himself to believe it. He took hold of the lid, raising it slowly at first, then threw it up with a yell of triumph.

The cry was choked off in his throat as the stink of rotting flesh swept over him and he staggered back in horror. Curled up in the chest was no piece of machinery – it was the dead body of Silvestro.

Leonardo stifled his fright and forced himself to take a closer look. The front of the artist's tunic was stained with dried blood, his skin pale, his eyes bulging. Leonardo reached out hesitantly to touch his cheek and felt cold flesh under his fingers.

It was obvious that Silvestro had been dead for some time, and it was equally obvious from the deep red stain over his breast that he had been killed by a single stab wound to the heart. Rodrigo's handiwork. Leonardo could not help glancing nervously around, as if the Spaniard might be lurking somewhere in the shadows, even though he had clearly committed this murder before setting out for Anchiano.

Silvestro was dead, the moulds destroyed, the diagram

removed, and Leonardo, who had seen it, was marked for death. This proved the importance Neroni attached to the machine. But how could Leonardo report this discovery to anyone when he was already wanted for murder himself? And what if he were found here with another body?

He slammed the lid shut and hurried back through Silvestro's study into the workshop. He was nearing the front door when he heard two familiar voices outside.

"What do you reckon's happened to old Silvestro then?"

"Lying on the floor of some tavern someplace, sleeping off one of his binges, I expect. We won't see him for days and then he won't remember nothing."

It was the artist's two apprentices and Leonardo knew they were sure to recognise him. As the door opened, he swerved and made a dash for the window.

"Hoy!" exclaimed Pimple-face. "Who's that?"

"It's him!" answered his friend. "The one that was dressed so fancy!"

Leonardo threw himself headlong at the open window, his arms stretched out before him. He hit the ground rolling and collided with a rain barrel. Ignoring the pain, he scrambled to his feet and took off at a run.

The two apprentices burst out of the front door in pursuit.

"Come back here! The Constable wants you!"

Leonardo dodged this way and that through the maze of narrow streets, moving too fast to have any idea where he was. Suddenly, he found himself below the looming walls of the church of Santo Spirito. At the far end of the street a dozen armed men were approaching.

Leonardo was sure that if they saw him running, they would stop him and ask his business, and he could hear the apprentices catching up behind him. He froze on the spot, unable to decide which way to go, which was the greater risk.

Just then four monks stepped out of the shadow of the church. They surrounded Leonardo, raising their arms in prayer so that their long sleeves flapped around him like sheets on a drying line.

"Walk with us," one of them hissed out of the side of his mouth, "and keep low."

Leonardo crouched down so that he was lost among the voluminous folds of the monks' grey robes as they walked, intoning Latin prayers as they went. He heard Silvestro's apprentices skid to a halt close by.

"Where's he gone then?"

"Burn his bones! There's a reward out for that sneak!"

The monks continued their solemn progress up the street while the apprentices continued to curse their ill luck. The armed men parted ranks before the brothers, bowing respectfully to them as they passed.

They rounded a corner into a small square where they halted and all turned inward to face Leonardo. Leonardo straightened up and tried to thank them, but the lead brother raised a hand to silence him.

"Are you Leonardo da Vinci, the pupil of Andrea del Verrocchio?" he asked.

Taken aback, Leonardo's first instinct was to lie. But surely, if he could not trust these holy men who had come to his rescue, there was no one he could trust.

"Yes, brother, I am," he answered. "But how do you know my name?"

All of the monks were staring at him intently and only now did he catch a glimpse of the faces under the shadow of their cowls. They were all bearded with hard, purposeful eyes, not the faces of holy men but of soldiers.

"Now!" the lead brother commanded.

Leonardo was immediately seized in an unbreakable grip. When he tried to cry out, a gag was stuffed into his mouth. Two of the brothers removed the cords from around their waists and used them to bind his arms to his sides. Another of them yanked a sack down over his head and shoulders.

Guided by the brothers, he stumbled blindly along the street. After a few moments, he heard the snort of a horse and the creak of wagon wheels. He was hoisted up and tossed into the back of the wagon. Someone hauled a sheet of canvas over him and then they were off.

Leonardo's stomach sank. Not only had he failed to find Silvestro's machine, but he had fallen into the hands of the enemy. There was little hope now that he would live to tell his tale.

20

A Man of Influence

There was a roll of thunder and the rain began pattering down on Leonardo's canvas covering. He struggled and twisted, trying to wriggle loose, but his bonds had been tied by men who were obviously used to this sort of work. His captors had said nothing to him since making him their prisoner, and they had said precious little to each other either.

There were two men up front driving, but all Leonardo heard out of them was an occasional grumble about the weather. Hoofbeats to the rear told him there were at least two more men riding escort, so that was all four of them accounted for.

They were not monks then, but what? Mercenaries? Bandits? Slavers? And where were they taking him? They had left the sounds of the city behind long ago, so they were not going to Pitti's palace – perhaps because it was safer to dispose of him elsewhere.

Finally, the wagon slowed to a halt and the canvas was stripped away. Leonardo could not tell if it was day or night, though he was sure they had been travelling for hours. He was dragged from the wagon and set down on a surface of wet cobbles. He could hear activity around him, muted voices, footsteps, doors being opened and closed.

Still without addressing him, one of his captors took him by the shoulder and steered him indoors. He felt wooden flooring beneath his feet and then the softness of an expensive carpet.

The sack was pulled away and the light of a dozen candles stung Leonardo's eyes. He was still blinking when a pair of servants entered the room, one carrying food and drink, the other a basin of water and some towels, and laid them out on the table.

The man who had brought him here removed the gag and the ropes. "Stay here and do not try to leave," he ordered. "The door will be guarded."

He ushered the servants out and locked the door after him.

Leonardo looked around at his prison. It was certainly a comfortable one, with two soft chairs and tapestries on the wall. The windows were high and barred and the rain was still drumming on the sill.

Whoever these people were, they appeared to be in no hurry to kill him. A pang of hunger reminded him that if he were to try to escape, he would need to keep his strength up. Walking over to the table, he washed his face and hands, drying himself off vigorously with the towel. Then he attacked the food with relish.

There was freshly baked bread, slices of honeyed ham, and partridge flavoured with quince jelly. The wine was the most delicious Leonardo had ever tasted. After the meal and two full cups, the tension and anxiety that had beset him all day gave way to irresistible fatigue. He sank into a chair and slipped into a deep, welcome slumber.

As he slept, his thoughts raced like multicoloured threads being whipped through the cogs and spools of a complex machine. He saw the diagram he had copied from Silvestro's workshop, so tantalising in its inscrutable detail. Then he saw the whole of the city of Florence laid out before him in the same way.

The city itself had become a machine, driven by the cogs and springs of the mysterious plan. The towers rose and fell in a complex sequence, the colossal dome of the cathedral was turning like a millwheel, and the streets were shifting back and forth like shuttles in a loom.

Then the relentless motion became a hand on his shoulder, shaking him awake. His eyes snapped open and he found himself staring into the face of Lorenzo de' Medici.

He jumped to his feet and Lorenzo backed off, raising his empty hands. "Easy, Leonardo. You are among friends here."

Lorenzo's hair and his riding clothes were damp from the rain. A sword with a silver hilt hung from his belt.

Leonardo was confused. "Where is here?"

"My father's villa at Careggi. I've been riding around our estates rousing our people to arms. When I got back, I was told you had arrived."

Leonardo laughed with relief. "I thought I had been taken by Neroni's men!"

"Before leaving Florence, I sent some of my most trusted men to protect you from Neroni," Lorenzo explained. "I described you to them, told them where you were headed and ordered them to bring you safely to me here."

"Why were they dressed up as monks?"

"My idea," said Lorenzo with a smile. "I did not think it

would be safe for them to enter the Oltrarno without a disguise, and the abbot of our local church owes me several favours. I'm sorry they treated you as they did. They were afraid you might be dangerous."

"They showed up just in time," said Leonardo. "I was caught between a flood and a fire when they appeared."

"Did you find what you were looking for?"

"No, something far worse: Silvestro's dead body. Rodrigo's work, I'd guess."

Lorenzo's eyes narrowed. "Matters grow more serious by the hour. Perhaps this will be enough to provoke my father to action."

Leonardo caught an undertone of frustration in Lorenzo's voice.

"He is ready to see you now and there is only a short while left before he retires for the night. I am afraid he will not stay up even a minute beyond his customary bedtime, no matter what the emergency."

Lorenzo led the way to a spacious room decorated with paintings and small statues of marble and bronze. A handful of trusted family members and allies were on hand, grouped on either side of Piero de' Medici.

Piero reclined like an invalid in a large chair padded with soft cushions. Beneath his pale, pouched face, his neck was puffed up like a toad's. His half-closed eyes and slouched posture gave him an air of fatigue. His clothes were as simple as that of any artisan, the only mark of his wealth being a ruby ring he wore on his liver-spotted right hand.

Leonardo was surprised. He knew Piero was referred to as 'Il Gottoso' because of his illness, but he had still expected someone more like the splendidly attired Luca Pitti or the tall, aristocratic Neroni. Instead, although he had all the things Leonardo's own father aspired to, Piero de' Medici flaunted none of them. When he spoke, it was in a soft, polite voice, not at all the regal tone of a powerful ruler.

"I apologise for keeping you waiting," he said. "When you arrived I was taking a sulphur bath to ease my joints. My health obliges me to dine early and my digestion forbids me to discuss business at table. I rely on a very strict routine to support me through the day, just as I rely on the support of my son."

He glanced over at Lorenzo and Leonardo could see the trust that bound father and son together. Piero returned his heavy-lidded eyes to his visitor, assessing him just as he would a customer seeking a loan from his bank. It was obvious that the burden of his illness had done nothing to blunt the sharpness of his wits.

"Lorenzo has given me a full account of your escapade at the Duomo," Piero continued. "I shall make a charitable donation to the church that will give honour to God and soothe the ruffled feelings of the bishop. Dealing with his brother, Diotisalvi Neroni, is another matter altogether."

"Fresina and I can testify that he was a party to murder," Leonardo pointed out.

"That may prove to be an effective bargaining counter later," said Piero, "but it does us no good right now."

"Can't you just have Neroni arrested?"

Piero pursed his lips. "How do you propose I do that? I am merely a private citizen who does not even hold public office."

"But I've heard that you are... that you have..." Leonardo hesitated. He realised from talking to Lorenzo earlier that it was ill-mannered – if not actually dangerous – to refer directly to Piero de' Medici as the ruler of Florence.

"I believe what you are trying to say is that I exercise a certain influence over the affairs of the city," Piero filled in for him dryly.

"Exactly," Leonardo agreed.

"Even if we accept that this is so, my recommendations

are unlikely to be followed if Neroni surrounds the Palace of the Signoria with armed men."

"And there is an army marching from Ferrara to help install Luca Pitti in power," Lorenzo reminded everyone.

"I have dispatched a messenger to the Duke of Milan humbly requesting his assistance in that regard," said Piero. "I believe he already has troops close to our borders. News of their approach should give the Duke of Ferrara pause."

"But that still leaves the armed mob Neroni has gathered at the Pitti Palace," said Lorenzo.

"The Signoria will shortly receive a letter," said Piero, "warning that the Ferrarese army is encamped at Pistoia, within easy striking distance of Florence. Under the circumstances, it will be my patriotic duty to arm the peasants who live on my estates and march them into the city to protect it from foreign attack. Once there, they will act as a deterrent to Neroni."

"Are we to have more bloodshed then?" asked Leonardo. He was suddenly haunted by memories of Tomasso and Silvestro, ruthlessly cut down as if they mattered no more than a couple of stalks of corn.

"Not if I can prevent it," said Piero. "Florence is like a sick man continually turning over in bed to avoid pain and never finding the right position. My duty, purely as a man who exercises a certain influence, is to keep the patient from falling out of bed and cracking his head on the floor."

The sun had scarcely cleared the horizon when Lorenzo set out on horseback on the road to Florence with Leonardo at his side. Too infirm to ride, Piero would follow later in a litter carried by six strong attendants.

Leonardo had discarded his peasant smock and replaced his straw hat with a proper cap which Lorenzo had provided. They trotted down the road southward with a single servant trailing behind. As they rode, Lorenzo spoke of his father.

"It is no small thing to be the guardian of the freedom of Florence for the sake of all her citizens. That freedom is a rare and precious thing in a world where most men live under the rule of kings and despots."

"But isn't your father just as much a sovereign as the princes and dukes who rule Milan, Ferrara and Naples?" Leonardo asked.

Lorenzo appeared to bristle at the suggestion, then his charming smile returned. "Absolutely not. He has no crown and no title. He is a citizen who must work for a living like everyone else. Have you seen the monument Luca Pitti is building for himself?"

"From a distance," Leonardo replied. "It's hard not to see it."

"The plans for that palace were originally submitted to my grandfather by Filippo Brunelleschi as the design for the new Medici town house he was intending to build. My grandfather rejected them, saying they were too grandiose for a simple banker. Instead, he built the more modest house we're on our way to now."

"But Pitti got hold of a copy of the plans and is building that palace for himself," said Leonardo.

"Correct," said Lorenzo. "So you see, my father does not live in a palace – and more importantly, he has no palace guard to enforce his will. If the citizens decide he is unfit to rule, they will turn against him and have the Signoria throw him out of the city."

Leonardo could not help but be aware of the affection and respect in Lorenzo's voice whenever he spoke of the elder Medici. How fortunate he was to have a father he could turn to in times of trouble, someone he could trust and who trusted him in return.

"One day, I suppose, it will be up to you to take over those responsibilities," said Leonardo.

A flicker of unease passed across Lorenzo's face. "I expect so, but I don't look forward to it. Governing Florence is no easy matter. You can see how it has destroyed my father's health. Personally I would rather be free to hunt, race my horses and write poetry." He gave Leonardo a grin. "Or even be a country boy playing in the fields and drawing pictures."

Leonardo was surprised that the rustic life was something Lorenzo could find desirable. It made him feel ashamed of having come to despise it so. "Well, when the time comes, can't you just refuse to be a leader?" he asked, shaking off his discomfiture.

Lorenzo cocked an eyebrow at him. "Do you think I could stand by and watch Florence collapse into chaos and mob rule? Or even worse, fall under the tyranny of a man like Neroni? No, my duty is to the city, not to my own wants. Even the deepest desire of my heart must be sacrificed to that end."

There was a catch in Lorenzo's voice and Leonardo realised he must be thinking of Lucrezia. At that moment, Leonardo found he no longer envied his companion. All of his wealth and privileges came at a price, and the course of his life had already been determined for him. Leonardo saw that if he had wished to, he could have followed the same career as his father. Or he could have chosen to become a farmer like his Uncle Franceso. And now, Maestro Andrea was offering him the chance to follow another path.

He could not help being just as ambitious as his father – he knew that now – but he could direct that ambition to a higher purpose than wealth or prestige.

The choice lay open to him.

The road took them over the crest of a hill. From the summit they could see the walls and rooftops of Florence in the distance below. The huge dome of the cathedral was clearly visible and the bell tower of the Palace of the Signoria. At the sight of it, Leonardo was reminded of his dream the previous day, then something more urgent seized his attention.

"Look!" he exclaimed, pointing. "There – among the trees close to that villa."

Lorenzo pulled up his horse and squinted. "My eyes are not as sharp as yours. What do you see?"

"Men and horses lurking in the shade. They look like they're waiting for something. One of them is on watch and I think he's spotted us."

Muscles tensed in Lorenzo's prominent jaw and he twisted the reins tightly around his fingers.

"An ambush, do you think?" Leonardo wondered aloud.

"Yes, but not for us. Neroni as good as told me he intends to have my father killed. It's a surer way to be rid of him than taking control of the Signoria."

"And then he would use Lucrezia as a hostage to drive you out of Florence," said Leonardo. "We should go back."

He started to turn his horse around.

Lorenzo grabbed his bridle. "No! As you say, they've spotted us already. If they see us leave, they will follow and my father's litter cannot outrun mounted pursuit."

He toyed with his sword hilt for a moment then turned and called back to his servant. "Domenico, stay back out of sight. There are armed men on the road ahead waiting to waylay Ser Piero. Ride back and warn him to take a different route."

Domenico promptly wheeled about and galloped off. Leonardo swallowed hard. "Shouldn't we go with him?"

"Not at all," said Lorenzo. "We need to make sure my father has time to reach safety."

"So what are we going to do?"

Lorenzo started his horse forward. "We're going to ride down there and pass the time of day with those fellows," he declared jauntily.

21

A Nest of Vipers

Soon they were close enough to discern the men clearly, even though they were still skulking among the trees. Lorenzo raised a hand and hailed them jovially. "Greetings, friends! Is this not a fine morning to be away from the noise and dust of the city?"

Leonardo held his breath, scarcely able to believe Lorenzo had the courage to be so casual with men who were waiting here to murder his father. There were six or seven of them, all armed with swords and daggers. Uncertain glances flashed back and forth between them until their leader stepped out of the shade.

Leonardo's first impulse was to turn and flee. It was the red-haired man who had stopped him in the Piazza della Signoria and asked him if he were for the Plain or the Hill. Unquestionably, he was one of Neroni's supporters. And if he should recognise Leonardo...

The red-haired man sauntered forward and eyed them insolently. "I recognise you. Aren't you Lorenzo de' Medici?"

"I am indeed," Lorenzo replied politely. "I regret I do not have the honour of knowing your name."

"My name is Luigi Circone. Is your father not with you?"

The question sent a cold shiver down Leonardo's back. If they turned and spurred their horses, might they yet be able to escape, he wondered.

"He is no more than an hour behind me," said Lorenzo with a smile. "You and your men must be the escort sent by the Signoria to accompany him into the city."

Circone grinned wolfishly. "That's exactly right."

"You've been waiting for some time. Perhaps I should ride back and hurry him along?" Lorenzo offered.

Circone raised a hand. "No need for that. It's still early in the day. And who is this with you?"

Leonardo's heart almost stopped. He lowered his head submissively and tugged his cap forward. "I'm merely a servant, sir," he mumbled.

Lorenzo quickly interposed. "Captain Circone, I can tell that you and your men are thirsty from your long vigil. Luckily, I have with me a flask of best Trebbiana wine, drawn from my father's private stock. You have never in your life tasted anything so sweet. Why don't we share it while we await him?"

"That would be most agreeable," said Circone, licking his lips at the prospect.

Cheerfully, Lorenzo dismounted and unhooked the large, leather wine flask from his saddle. Quaking at the risk they were taking, Leonardo climbed down from his own horse and joined the assassins in the shade of the trees. He felt as if he were sitting down in the middle of a nest of vipers, any one of whom might suddenly turn and bite.

The next half hour was the longest Leonardo had experienced in his entire life. Lorenzo, on the other hand, seemed utterly at home, laughing and joking as if he were in the company of his closest friends.

At once point he even launched into a song:

"The ladies of Tuscany
Everyone knows
Will sell you a kiss
For the price of a rose.

But roses must wither
And kisses will fade,
So save your last rose
For the next pretty maid."

His cracked, high-pitched voice had Circone and his men guffawing as much as the bawdy lyrics. One of them gave Leonardo a jovial thump on the back. He did his best to join in the merriment while trying to remain as inconspicuous as possible.

Just when he was beginning to think the worst was over, Circone suddenly stared him in the face. "I know you, don't I, boy?"

"I don't think so," Leonardo said. "I don't recognise anybody here."

Circone frowned, clearly unconvinced.

Once again, Lorenzo came to the rescue. "Captain, you have stopped drinking!" He thrust the wineskin under Circone's nose. Soon the two of them were warbling a drinker's song in loud, broken voices.

Leonardo felt as though an axe had been removed from his neck. Just then Lorenzo looked up at the hill from which they had spotted the ambush.

"Look there!" he exclaimed. "Here comes my father now!"

Circone and his men blearily scanned the hillside for some sign of their victim.

Lorenzo scurried over to his horse. Seizing the reins, he jumped into the saddle. "Come along!" he called to Leonardo. "We must ride on ahead and prepare a proper welcome. Good luck to you, Captain Circone!"

Leonardo barely had time to mount his horse before Lorenzo was galloping up the road towards Florence.

"What did you see up there?" he asked once he had caught up.

Lorenzo chuckled. "I didn't see anything. I just needed to distract those cut-throats while we made our getaway. If their eyes were as keen as yours, they would have seen through the deception. By the time they realise they've been tricked, we'll be safe inside the city walls. And so will my father."

They entered Florence by the Porta Faenza and made their way through the increasingly crowded streets to the Via Larga and the Medici house. It was an impressive, three-storey building that surrounded a wide courtyard. Lorenzo led the way through the open gateway beneath the Medici emblem of six circles set on a shield.

"What is that symbol supposed to be?" Leonardo asked.

"The story goes back to our ancestor, the knight Averardo," Lorenzo replied. "He was fighting a giant who had been terrorising the countryside around here. When the battle was over, the giant was dead, but his club had left six huge dents in Averardo's shield."

"It doesn't sound very likely," said Leonardo.

"That's what my father thinks," said Lorenzo as they dismounted. "He prefers to think of those circles as coins, since that is more suitable for a family of bankers. Personally, I prefer the old tale."

Servants and retainers rushed to greet their young master and take care of the horses. Once they had assured him that his father had arrived unharmed, Lorenzo swept Leonardo off to the dining hall where Ser Piero was poised to address a gathering of his supporters.

The head of the Medici family was standing, in spite of his illness. A map of the city was spread out on the table before him. Behind him, frescoes of biblical prophets decorated the wall and facing them were statues of Roman deities perched on pedestals between the high windows. Members of the household were gathered on all sides, some of them wearing breastplates with swords at their sides.

A smile lit Piero's sallow face when his son entered the room. "Lorenzo, I have been worried to distraction. Where have you been all this time?"

"I was sharing wine and song with the welcoming committee Neroni sent out to meet you," Lorenzo replied jokingly. "They are actually rather jolly company, for murderers."

"I imagine they are a lot less jolly now they know they have been tricked," said Leonardo.

Lorenzo delivered a brief account of their adventure. Piero was obviously torn between admiration for his son and horror at the risk he had taken.

"From now on we cannot afford to take such chances," he said. "The first of our troops from the country are already arriving. We must close off all the gates into the northern part of the city" – with his forefinger he stabbed where the gates were marked on the map – "leaving only the Porta San Gallo for our reinforcements. Rubeo, is our warning about the Ferrarese army on its way to the Signoria?"

Piero's clerk nodded.

"Will they believe it, do you think?" asked Lorenzo.

"I don't care if they believe it or not," said Piero. "I have informed them that I am organising the defence of the city.

That is what counts. Now, what word do we have of Neroni?"

A sergeant-at-arms stepped forward. "He has mustered up to 200 men at the Pitti Palace. To all intents and purposes, the Oltrarno has become a separate city under Luca Pitti's rule."

Piero allowed himself a rueful smile. "That pompous idiot. He has what he has always wanted – his own little kingdom right on his doorstep. He will make that palace of his bigger than the Colosseum at Rome, if he doesn't run out of money first."

There was a ripple of laughter. Piero singled out three of his most trusted servants. "I want you to send men around to every wine shop, butcher and baker in Florence. Buy up every scrap of food and every drop of wine in the city."

"But the expense!" one of the servants exclaimed.

"Use however much money it takes," Piero insisted. "There has to be some advantage to owning a bank."

"But, Father, shouldn't we be buying weapons?" Lorenzo objected.

"In good time," said Piero, "but right now we need the people behind us. If you were a common citizen, who would you rather support: the man who expects you to fight or the man who offers you as much food and wine as your belly can hold?"

Just then a grimace of pain twisted Piero's face and he sank into his large padded chair. "Lorenzo, you must see to the defence of the house," he said. "Luca Pitti will act cautiously, I believe, but Neroni might take it into his head to attack us here."

"If we don't attack him first," Lorenzo suggested with an eager gleam in his eye.

"Put such nonsense out of your mind," Piero ordered through tight lips. "I will not be the one to strike the first blow and start bloodshed on the streets."

"But Lucrezia—" Lorenzo began.

"Lucrezia will keep. This is a time for careful steps, not grand gestures."

Lorenzo looked crestfallen as his father turned to another of his manservants. "To you, Giorgio, falls the most important task of all. You must ensure that lunch and supper are served exactly on time, as usual. I will not put my digestion at the mercy of my enemies."

Lorenzo marched out of the room with Leonardo at his heels. "How can he expect me to just sit here and do nothing?" he muttered in frustration.

A bearded man with the bearing of a soldier was waiting

for his young master at the end of the passage. Leonardo recognised him as one of the monks who had abducted him in the Oltrarno.

"Bartolomeo, I need a full inventory of all the weapons we have in store," Lorenzo ordered. "And fetch beams from the basement. We'll use them to brace the doors in case of attack."

"At once," Bartolomeo said gruffly.

"I will have one of our scribes take a statement from you to be presented to the Signoria at the proper time," Lorenzo said to Leonardo. "In the mean time, you have the run of the house."

He walked off briskly with Bartolomeo.

Leonardo could not help feeling redundant in the midst of all the activity. He felt the folded paper still secure under his tunic and cursed himself for being unable to understand it.

He walked out into the courtyard where the bright sunshine stabbed his eyes. All around, servants and soldiers were bustling about with sacks, boxes, spears and swords.

"Leonardo! Leonardo!" called a voice.

Turning, Leonardo saw Sandro and Fresina hurrying towards him. Sandro embraced him and beamed.

"Leonardo, where have you been? When you didn't come back from the Duomo, I feared the worst."

Leonardo explained about Silvestro's workshop and what had happened after. Fresina tutted and took a bite from the chicken leg she held in her hand. "You were a fool to act the burglar without my help," she said as she chewed. "It is only to be expected that you would be caught."

"She's been practising her skills in the Medici kitchens," said Sandro despairingly.

"But how do you two come to be here?" Leonardo asked.

"Men came and said they were taking us to safety," said Fresina, wiping grease from her chin with the back of her hand. "I wanted to fight, but Sandro said no." She gave Sandro a contemptuous look.

"I recognised one of them from my visit to the Medici house," Sandro explained. "I had to wrest my palette knife away from her to avoid a bloodbath."

"When I got here," said Fresina, "they bundled me into a room and made me tell my story to a scribe. He kept far away from me like I smelled" – she pinched her nose between two fingers and grinned maliciously – "so I spoke very quiet so he could not hear me without coming close. He wrote everything down in very small letters and had me sign it with my mark. Then he told me to go, like the smell had got worse."

A servant carrying a bench on his shoulder bumped Leonardo as he blundered past. "Isn't there somewhere quiet we can go?" Leonardo complained.

"I know just the place," Sandro declared. "Follow me."

He led the way through an archway into a lavish garden surrounded by a covered walkway. Several finely sculpted biblical figures stood in a circle around an ornate fountain from which a stream of sparkling water arced into the air. Leonardo scooped some water up in his hands and splashed his face.

Fresina tossed the bare chicken bone into a flowerbed and sucked the fat from her fingers. "You are not the only bad thief in this city," she said to Leonardo, as she plunged her hands into the water. "The kitchen maids told me two burglars broke into this house last night."

"Burglars?" Leonardo was instantly alert.

"Yes, a servant saw them run off carrying a heavy sack," said Fresina, wiping her hands dry on the front of her smock. "A good thief should never be seen. In Circassia they would be dishonoured."

"What did they take?" Sandro asked.

"That is an even greater dishonour," said Fresina

disapprovingly. "The whole house was searched and nothing was found to be missing. What is the point in stealing something no one will miss?"

"Nothing missing?" Leonardo said. *Nothing missing.*

The words rang in his head like the clanging of a bell. His thoughts flew back to his dream, of the whole city moving like a machine, and in the centre the great dome of the cathedral revolving like a vast wheel.

"That's it!" he exclaimed. "I have the answer at last!"

22

A Choice of Angels

Leonardo knelt down in front of a marble bench and spread his drawing out over it. "Silvestro told me that whatever I had seen, it would do me no good. Why do you think he said that?"

"I don't know, Leonardo," Sandro sighed. "I was never much for riddles."

"Because he knew that what I'd seen was exactly what Toscanelli saw – a machine that would not function."

Fresina flopped down on the bench beside the drawing. "You are raving, Leonardo. All your adventures have made you crooked in the head." She patted herself on the brow.

“No, I was crooked in the head before. I wasn’t thinking straight, but now it seems so obvious. There’s something missing from the drawing.”

“Why?” Sandro asked.

“So that no one else could build the machine from this diagram. But Silvestro himself knew what was missing and could correct it during the construction. The whole point of the trick is that it is so simple. It’s as easy as standing an egg on its end.”

Recalling his dream once more, the dome turning slowly in the centre of the city, Leonardo knew exactly what it was that Silvestro had left out. He picked a stick of charcoal from the pouch at his belt and sketched into the centre of the diagram a large notched wheel.

“You see, if the components of the machine are brought together, the smaller cogs will fit their teeth into this large one, the moving rods will connect and the whole machine will move as it is supposed to.”

“It is still nothing but lines and circles,” said Fresina.

“No, it’s much more than that now,” said Leonardo as he carefully ran his index finger around the completed diagram. “This coil is wound and held in check until this catch here is pressed. Then the motion begins like a clock, the movement being passed from one side of the device to the other through the central wheel. Notch by notch, the cogs turn until at last, at some predetermined time, the weight drops, the larger spring is released…"

Sandro craned over Leonardo's shoulder. "And?"

"The force of it makes this bar here jump forward."

"To what end?"

Leonardo stared at the drawing. "I don't know, but a spring this large would deliver a mighty blow to whatever was in the way. Perhaps it strikes a bell or a gong."

Sandro blinked. "That hardly seems worth all the fuss."

Leonardo gritted his teeth and squeezed the charcoal between his fingers until it snapped. Sandro was right. If anything, he was now more baffled than ever.

"Hsst! Someone is coming," warned Fresina.

Leonardo got up and stuffed the drawing back into his tunic as a tall, bony individual stalked into the garden. He was dressed in the finery of a valued servant and had a sheaf of papers under his arm. He turned his small, probing eyes on Leonardo.

"You are Leonardo da Vinci?"

"The last time somebody asked me that," said Leonardo, "they tied me up and pulled a sack over my head."

Fresina pinched her nose at the man and he sniffed

disdainfully. Leonardo guessed this was the scribe she had been speaking about earlier.

"I have been instructed to write down your account of the unfortunate events at the Torre Donati," the man said.

"In that case, I am Leonardo da Vinci," said Leonardo, following the scribe out of the garden.

Throughout the day the Medici house was a hive of frantic activity. Supplies were delivered and packed into the storerooms. Men streamed in from the country armed with pitchforks and spears. Companies were hastily assembled and marched off to patrol the nearby streets or guard the city gates.

While Piero dispatched letters to potential allies and foreign ambassadors, Lorenzo saw that the doors and windows were barricaded against attack and set lookouts on the rooftops. Midway through the afternoon a messenger arrived with the news that the Signoria had shut themselves up in their palace and barred the doors. A mob of Luca Pitti's supporters had marched around the Piazza della Signoria chanting slogans, before retreating back over the bridges to the Oltrarno.

All Leonardo and Sandro could do was try to stay out of the way. Eventually, they took refuge in the library. Sandro gazed wide-eyed at the array of works that crowded the shelves.

"I had no idea the Medici were such scholars!" he exclaimed. "I'll wager there's no collection like this outside of the papal vaults in Rome! And have you seen the works of art they have all over the house? There are some of Donatello's greatest masterpieces here."

Leonardo could not share his friend's enthusiasm. Nothing in the Medici house held even a fraction of the interest Silvestro's diagram did. He had the drawing laid out before him again, studying how the cogs, wheels, shafts and springs interlocked, asking himself again and again what could be the final result of all this ingenuity.

Outside in the courtyard the babble of voices mixed with the rasp of grindstones on steel and the clip-clop of horses' hooves. Leonardo dragged his fingers through his hair, as if trawling for some insight.

"All these preparations for battle are useless!" he burst out. "Whatever Neroni is planning, it can't be stopped by an army!"

Sandro looked up from a manuscript. "Why don't you put that away! I swear you're letting it drive you mad. Let me read you some of this. It's about the siege of Troy and the wooden horse."

"I can't sit here listening to stories. I need to do something."

"We're artists, Leonardo, not soldiers. There's nothing we can do."

Leonardo snatched up the drawing and headed for the door. "At the very least I can find Lorenzo and tell him what I've discovered."

"Which isn't very much," Sandro reminded him as he stormed out of the library, slamming the door shut behind him.

Leonardo asked around after Lorenzo and was directed to the exercise room in the west wing of the house. As he opened the door he heard the harsh clatter of steel striking steel. He saw before him a long room, the walls lined with ropes and bars. Benches, beams and leather balls were laid out on the floor in such a way as to leave a clear aisle up the centre.

It was here that Lorenzo and Bartolomeo were exchanging quick, precise sword blows. They advanced and retreated in turn, striking out in a rhythmic series of expertly timed moves.

Leonardo understood that this was an exercise, a prearranged sequence designed to sharpen the fencer's reflexes. However, he doubted the exercise was usually performed with the vehemence Lorenzo was displaying. Bartolomeo stolidly met each furious blow, allowing his young master to vent his frustration in this mock combat.

There was a final flurry of steel, then Lorenzo tossed his sword aside and snatched up a wet towel to wipe the perspiration from his face. He had stripped off his tunic and his light, open-necked shirt was stained with sweat from his exertions. Only when he laid the towel aside did he become aware of Leonardo.

"You look well prepared for a fight," Leonardo complimented him.

Lorenzo gave a hollow laugh. "This is as close as I will get to a fight if my father has his way. He says that by nightfall we will have more men under arms than Neroni, but he still will not allow me to go after Lucrezia."

"Your father is a cautious man," Bartolomeo commented quietly. "He hopes to resolve this business without blood."

Lorenzo's eyes flashed. "Do you know what he did?" he asked Leonardo. "He made me swear by all the saints and the Blessed Virgin that I would not attempt to rescue Lucrezia." He stretched out his arms and pressed his wrists together. "I might as well be manacled!"

He slumped down on the nearest bench and pressed a fist to his mouth.

Leonardo recalled his first sight of Lorenzo. He had wondered what Lucrezia could find to love in one so plain and graceless. Since then he had seen Lorenzo ride into the midst of a band of assassins to save his father. Now he was equally prepared to risk his life for Lucrezia's sake.

Leonardo was embarrassed to think that his own concern had been with solving a puzzle, with demonstrating his own brilliance. But perhaps there was still something he could do to help. He recalled something Lorenzo had told him on the journey from Careggi and it suggested a plan to him.

"Your father is correct that an armed assault on Pitti's palace would do more harm than good," he said. "But where an army might fail, one man might succeed through stealth."

Lorenzo looked up sharply. "You think so?"

"It's surely the last thing Neroni would expect," said Leonardo.

"It is true that surprise is the greatest weapon of all," Lorenzo agreed, jumping to his feet.

"But Pitti's palace is vast," Bartolomeo objected. "A man could lose his own shadow in that maze of rooms. How could he find a prisoner and make his escape?"

"He would need a map," said Leonardo matter-of-factly.

"And I think we may have one. Lorenzo, didn't you say that Pitti's palace is based upon designs submitted to your family."

"Yes, and rejected by my grandfather Cosimo."

"But might you still have a copy of those plans?"

A gleam of hope flashed in Lorenzo's eyes. "We just might at that! Father never throws anything away. If the plans still exist, they will be stored in the library."

When the library door burst open, Sandro jumped from his chair with a yelp. He settled back with a groan of relief when he saw it was only Lorenzo and Leonardo, not some invading enemy. Lorenzo stalked around the room, his eyes darting this way and that, like a hunter in search of his prey. He stopped at a wide set of drawers and began rummaging through them with furious determination.

"What is going on?" Sandro asked, alarmed by Lorenzo's behaviour.

Leonardo explained about the floor plans and Sandro groaned. "Must there always be some wild scheme with you? Can't we just sit peacefully to one side and let events take their course?"

Lorenzo closed the first drawer with a growl and started on the second. This too he slammed shut, his dark brows knotted in impatience. He yanked open the next drawer and continued his search.

"Plans for the villas at Careggi and Cafaggiolo," he muttered. "The chapel at San Lorenzo... Here it is! Filippo Brunelleschi – plans for the proposed Medici Palace."

He hauled out a roll of parchment and tossed it on to the nearest table. Leonardo and Sandro joined him. Untying the bundle, Lorenzo separated it into three large sheets and unrolled the first.

Leonardo swept his gaze over the page. Here was the layout of the ground floor: vestibule, storage rooms, reception chambers, with all the passages and stairways clearly marked. Lorenzo unrolled the second and the third, laying them on top of each other. Bedrooms, galleries, banqueting halls. Leonardo took in every detail.

Lorenzo studied the plans in his turn. "Well, it is a map, I suppose," he said doubtfully, "but no one could possibly sneak into Pitti's palace carrying all this."

"He could if he was carrying it here," said Leonardo. He tapped his index finger against his temple.

"But there is no time to memorise all these details," Lorenzo objected. "In a couple of hours it will be dark."

"I don't need much time," said Leonardo, his eyes still fixed on the plans.

"It's true," Sandro confirmed. "He draws things in his

mind and keeps them there. But, Leonardo, how can you be sure Pitti has followed the exact layout of these plans?"

Leonardo found himself thinking of his father. "If Luca Pitti is as vain and envious as they say, he will want to live in exactly the palace the Medici considered too grand for themselves. That is what a vain and empty man would do."

Lorenzo leaned his weight against the table and stared hard at Leonardo. "You're volunteering to take this mission on yourself?"

Leonardo had finished memorising the first of the sheets and was now on to the second. "There's no one else who can do it," he replied. "I can keep this map in my head and Lucrezia knows me."

Lorenzo ground his teeth. "I wish I could come with you."

"Even if your father allowed it, your face is too well known," said Leonardo.

"The bridges over the Arno will be guarded by Neroni's men," Sandro pointed out. "What makes you think they'll let you pass?"

Leonardo summoned what he hoped was a convincing smile. "If the Medici have bought up all the food and wine in Florence, who's going to turn away a wagon loaded with both?"

Lorenzo nodded. "Yes, I shall arrange it." He fixed Leonardo with a searching gaze. "This is not a favour I would willingly ask of anyone, not even one of my own family."

Leonardo recalled what Maestro Andrea had told him, about the angels who refused to join the war in Heaven and how they had lost their wings as a result. "It's not a matter of favours," he said. "It's a matter of choosing sides."

23

THE UNHOLY MOUNTAIN

Leonardo wrapped a grey cloak round his shoulders and yanked the hood up over his head. Underneath he wore the garb of a servant of a wealthy household, which was what he would pretend to be once he reached the Pitti Palace. Then he headed out into the courtyard where Lorenzo and Sandro were waiting by the wagon.

"My father took some persuading to go along with this plan," Lorenzo said. "He only agreed on condition that absolutely no one else be involved. I'm to warn you that if you're caught, he will disclaim all knowledge of you."

"I understand," said Leonardo.

"Good luck," said Sandro, giving his friend a quick embrace. "I'll be praying for your safe return."

"Don't worry," Leonardo joked. "I'm the Lion of Anchiano, remember?"

"You should have a sword," Lorenzo said. "Let me give you this." He began to unbuckle his own sword belt.

"No, keep it," said Leonardo. "It would just make me more conspicuous. Besides, I don't know how to use one."

Lorenzo clasped him firmly by the hand. "I am sending you in my place to do what I would dearly wish to do myself," he said. He reached inside his tunic and brought out a small brooch fashioned from gold with three rubies in the centre. "Give this to Lucrezia," he said, "and she will know I have sent you."

Leonardo found his voice catching as he accepted the brooch and tucked it away in a pouch. "You stood against Neroni to protect me," he said. "I will try to be worthy of that, for your sake and Lucrezia's."

He clambered up into the wagon and flicked the reins. The two stout horses started forward, hauling their load through the open gateway and out into the Via Larga. Night was falling over the city and it seemed unnaturally quiet. Few would risk setting foot outside their homes while two armed camps stood ready to turn Florence into a battlefield.

The hoofbeats of the horses echoed emptily off the walls as Leonardo passed the church of San Lorenzo. Suddenly, a figure appeared from the shadows and scurried towards him. Without breaking stride, Fresina gripped the side of the wagon and swung herself up on to the seat beside him.

Leonardo reined the horses in sharply. "Fresina, what are you doing here?"

"I knew Il Gottoso was not allowing anyone to go with you, so I sneaked out and hid till you came by." She hunched over and darted her eyes furtively from side to side.

"I don't want anyone else along – you least of all," said Leonardo. "Aren't you in enough trouble already?"

Fresina folded her arms and scowled like a thundercloud. "I know that you will need my help, so here I am."

"Why should I need your help?"

"Because you do not know my mistress," Fresina replied. "You only know brushes and paint."

Leonardo shook his head. "You would be taking a terrible risk."

"It is my risk to choose," Fresina insisted. "I told you my mistress did me a kindness, and that I will not forget."

Leonardo thought for a long moment, seeing the

determination in the girl's face and in the stubborn set of her shoulders. Her mind was made up as surely as his own, and perhaps for better reasons.

"Very well," he said, "but stay close to me the whole time, and do only what I tell you to do."

He gave the reins a flick and the wagon rolled southward through the darkening streets. They passed the stores of the wool merchants on the Via Calimara and the warehouses of the clothmakers.

On the Ponte Vecchio the butchers, tanners and blacksmiths were shutting up shop for the day. The wagon rolled past them over the river. On the far side stood a band of men who were lighting lanterns and keeping watch for any sign of an attack by the Medici.

"Do you think they will know us?" Fresina whispered.

"There's no reason why they should. After all, we're the last people on earth anyone would expect to come calling on Luca Pitti."

A man stepped out in front of them, hefting a lantern up above his head. "Ho! What is this you have in your wagon?"

Leonardo reined in the horses and smiled innocently. "Meat, bread and many casks of wine to be delivered to the Pitti Palace."

"The palace? Do you have a written order?"

"No, but I was told the noble Luca Pitti himself had sent for these goods. He is planning a victory banquet for his followers."

The man walked around the wagon, lifting the covers from the baskets and sniffing at their contents.

"You had best let him through, Carlo," said one of his companions. "There will be hell to pay if anyone finds out we held up their food."

"All right, go ahead," said the first man gruffly. As Leonardo started the horses moving again he shouted after him, "Be sure and tell them to send a change of watch. We're not standing here starving all night while they stuff themselves."

"I'll remember that," Leonardo called back.

As the wagon drew away, Fresina said, "You lie like a Circassian."

"Is that good?"

"It is very good. It gives me confidence. A man who cannot lie well cannot do anything well."

Soon the square bulk of the Pitti Palace rose up imposingly before them. It was forty feet high, built from four-ton blocks of stone that had been cut from the hillside that rose up behind the grandiose structure. Florence had never seen anything like it. It was as though Luca Pitti had raised up a mountain, a personal Olympus, within the walls of the city.

The arched windows – all of them bigger than the main doors of the Medici house – were ablaze with yellow light. In the forecourt, bands of men were gathered around braziers, the glimmer of the coals reflecting ruddily from steel blades and polished shields.

The arrival of the wagon drew immediate attention. A man in a crimson cloak and plumed helmet signalled Leonardo to stop, and a circle of men formed around them.

"What's this, fresh supplies?" said the man in the helmet. "I wasn't informed of this. Who authorised it?"

"Ser Luca Pitti arranged it," Leonardo said confidently.

"Is that so?" queried a lofty voice.

The crowd parted to make way for a grand figure in a fur-lined cloak, a gold-hilted sword hanging at his side. Leonardo recognised the man instantly as the one he and Sandro had seen riding in procession past the Duomo the previous day.

It was Luca Pitti, the Saviour of Florence.

"You say I ordered all of this?" Pitti asked, eyeing the packed wagon uncertainly.

Leonardo decided to stake everything on Pitti's

notorious vanity. "No doubt you delegated one of your underlings to deal with it," he answered. "Naturally, you are far too busy a man to attend to such details personally."

He raised his voice so that all those who were crowding round could hear him clearly. "This is the very best of food and the sweetest of wine," he proclaimed. "What else is worthy of the heroic defenders of Florence? And who else but Luca Pitti would be so generous as to provide it all at his own expense?"

A huge cheer went up. Pitti's face flushed with satisfaction at the approval of his men. That was clearly more important to him than the details of how these supplies had come to be delivered.

Fresina leaned close. "It is true," she whispered. "He is a vain fool."

"These goods had best be taken to the kitchens," Leonardo announced, setting the wagon in motion.

Pitti's voice rang out sharply. "Stop!"

Men moved to block Leonardo's way and the wagon came to a halt. Pitti wove his way through the ranks and grabbed him by the wrist.

"Not so fast, my young friend," he said.

Leonardo's heart pounded. His mouth was dry as dust.

If Pitti had seen through the deception, there was no way they could escape.

He felt something being pressed into his palm. He looked down and saw a coin, a five *soldi* piece.

"Take this for your trouble," said Luca Pitti with a benevolent smile.

Releasing his grip on Leonardo, he waved the wagon on and turned to acknowledge the applause of his men.

The officer in the plumed helmet beckoned a dozen men forward. "Come on, lads!" he urged them. "The sooner we get these viands unloaded, the sooner we eat!"

"And drink!" added another with a chortle.

Noisily, they closed in around Leonardo and Fresina. The man in the helmet personally led the wagon through an arch to the kitchen entrance. Here the men started hauling casks and baskets down from the wagon and ferrying them indoors.

Leonardo and Fresina climbed down from the driving seat. "What now?" Fresina asked.

Leonardo looked up at the wall of the Pitti Palace with its rough stonework looming over them like a cliff face. "It's time to enter the lion's den," he said.

He and Fresina took a basket each and joined the line of men filing into the kitchen. Inside, the hubbub of voices mingled with the sizzle and sputter of roasting meat and the clang of pots and spoons.

Pheasant and guinea fowl revolved on loaded spits and cauldrons of pasta bubbled on the open hearth. Firelight glistened on copper pans and pewter tankards. The air, heavy with steam and drifting clouds of flour, was shot through with the pungent scent of spices and the sweet smell of baking bread.

Servants stood at long tables, washing vegetables and carving up slices of lamb and roast beef. Others were bustling this way and that with buckets of water and bowls of herbs. In the midst of them, a florid-faced cook was waving his arms frantically at the new arrivals, who crowded in with their bundles of produce.

"What is this? Fresh supplies? Why did no one warn me?"

"It is not possible to anticipate the generosity of the noble Luca Pitti," said Leonardo, weaving his way through the congestion.

"No, no, you fools, carry it over there!" the cook cried in exasperation. "And the wine goes through that door there – to the cellar! No, the other door! Mules! Donkeys!"

Fresina plucked a rosy apple from a salver. Instantly, the cook stretched over and snatched it from her hand as though it were a purse full of gold florins.

He wagged an angry finger at her. "There is no eating in the kitchen, only cooking!" He rounded on one of the men who was lurching past him with a tub of onions. "Imbecile! Watch out for that pot!"

Fresina's eyes flickered towards another apple. Leonardo pulled her away. "Here take this," he said, shoving a tray into her hands.

A man squeezed past and set a cask of wine on a nearby table. Leonardo plucked up a flagon, filled it from the bung and sat it on the tray.

"Hey, what are you up to?" the cook demanded.

"Ser Luca Pitti has ordered me to take wine to his honoured guest Lucrezia Donati," Leonardo explained innocently.

The cook scowled at him. "Who are you? I don't know you from a pig's behind."

"With all these people gathered here, Ser Luca has had to take on extra staff," Leonardo explained. "I am Luigi Pangini from the village of Cafaggiolo. My father is the blacksmith there and can bend a horseshoe with his bare hands. My grandfather was—"

"Enough, idiot!" the cook sputtered impatiently. "I don't want your family history. Take the wine and be gone.

And don't forget to take cups for Signora Pitti and her daughter."

"Oh, are they keeping their guest company?" said Leonardo airily. "Where exactly are they entertaining her?"

"Can I have no peace?" the cook exclaimed. "They are in the Peacock Chamber. Do you know where that is or do I have to lead you by the hand like a blind man?"

"It's on the third floor," said Leonardo, "to the east. I can find it easily."

"Good. Then go!" The cook turned and yelled over at the far side of the kitchen. "Armando, you simpleton! The sauce – it is boiling over! Stir it! Stir it!"

Leonardo plucked three cups from a shelf and placed them on the tray. He snapped his fingers under Fresina's nose. "Come, girl. Follow me," he commanded.

They hurried out into a passage and walked briskly away. It was strangely quiet after the uproar of the kitchen.

"That fat fool, could he not see I was hungry?" Fresina exclaimed in disgust.

"Forget about food," said Leonardo, tugging her sleeve. "We don't have time."

"That is not so easy – I can still smell it," said Fresina, sniffing. "Do you know where you are going?"

"Of course. I've memorised the plans of this palace. How do you think I knew the way to the kitchen?"

Fresina was unimpressed. "The captain led us there."

"Well, trust me, I can get to the room where they are keeping Lucrezia."

Suddenly, a coarse voice came echoing down the empty passage. "I knew it! We're lost!"

"No, we're not," said a second voice. "I know exactly where we are."

Leonardo saw two scruffily dressed youths strolling towards them. He recognised them at once. Pimple-face and the Twitcher!

There was nowhere to hide and if he turned back now it would look suspicious. Like Lorenzo, he would have to be bold and head straight into the danger. He yanked up his hood and hunched forward to hide his face.

"Walk quickly!" he whispered to Fresina.

Together they strode briskly up the passage as if on an urgent errand.

"The kitchen's down this way," Pimple-face was saying, "and they just had a load of grub delivered."

"Do you think we should sample it, just to make sure it's not rotten?" Twitcher suggested.

While they convulsed with laughter at their joke,

Leonardo ducked past. As Fresina went by, Pimple-face Suddenly called out, "Hang on, girly, what's that you got there?"

24

Into the Darkness

"Wine," Fresina answered curtly.

Leonardo slowed and risked a backward glance. He could not stop in case the apprentices recognised him.

"Spare a drop for a poor working man, my little beauty," Twitcher pleaded in a mocking tone. He tried to put an arm around Fresina's shoulders, but she drove him off with a kick to the shins.

"It is not for you, flea-bitten dogs!" she shrilled at them. "It is for my mistress. And if you try to lay a hand on me again, I will put the curse of a thousand sores upon you!"

She half-turned her head and fixed one baleful eye

upon them. She was huffing like an enraged bull.

Pimple-face plucked at his friend's sleeve. "Best steer clear of that one," he advised. "She's got the look of a witch."

"You're right," Twitcher agreed. A nervous tick tugged the side of his mouth. "We can get plenty of wine without her." The two apprentices backed away carefully then turned and scuttled off towards the kitchen.

Fresina caught up with Leonardo. "You know them?"

Leonardo nodded. "I couldn't take the chance they would recognise me."

"Pah!" Fresina spat contemptuously. "You should not have worried. They have the bodies of men but the souls of maggots."

Leonardo stopped to consult the map in his head and moved on. The further they went, the more concentrated effort it took to match what he saw before him with the abstract diagrams he had seen at the Medici house.

He wasn't helped by the fact that work on the palace was not yet completed. Some of the corridors were littered with ladders, scaffolding, sacks of plaster and tubs of paint. It looked as if the workmen had abandoned their labours to join the brewing festivities. However, once he had made allowances for that, Leonardo found that the layout was exactly as he had expected.

"Filippo planned every detail of this place, right down to the decoration of the rooms," he said. "Luckily for us, Luca Pitti has followed his instructions like a holy man follows the commandments of God."

Occasionally, they passed a member of the household or a wandering soldier, but everyone was too busy to pay any attention to a pair of humble servants. They could hear songs being sung in front of the palace. Spirits were running high and the atmosphere was one of imminent victory for Luca Pitti and his friends.

They headed down a brightly painted gallery. Leonardo counted the doors and pointed to the third one on the right, which was painted with the image of a peacock. They approached stealthily, keeping their eyes peeled for anyone coming from either direction. From inside the room they could hear the buzz of female voices.

"What will you do about Pitti's womenfolk?" Fresina asked darkly. "Kill them?"

"Of course not. But we must get them out of there before Lucrezia has a chance to raise the alarm. After all, she may still believe we're a pair of murderers."

"If only we were!" said Fresina with feeling. "How much simpler things would be."

"Put the tray down by the door and wait out of sight," Leonardo instructed her. "As soon as the Pitti women come out, run in and shut the door after you."

He drew himself up and straightened his tunic. Then he took a deep breath and barged into the room.

A plump woman sat on a divan with her round-faced daughter. To their left Lucrezia sat in a chair. All three of them had embroidery in their laps, but their needles froze in position when the door banged open.

"Signora Pitti!" Leonardo cried. "Your husband has been taken gravely ill! He is crying out for you!"

The plump woman jumped to her feet, her needlework tumbling to the floor. "Ill you say? Where is he?"

Leonardo let his voice rise to a panic-stricken shriek. "In the banqueting hall, at the other end of the palace."

Lucrezia and the daughter also sprang up. Lucrezia stared at Leonardo in bewilderment.

"What is he doing in the banqueting hall?" asked the daughter.

"Never mind that!" her mother scolded sharply. "We must go to him at once."

They both bustled out of the door in a flurry of silks. The instant they were gone, Fresina bounded in and slammed the door shut.

Lucrezia staggered back, knocking over her chair. Her eyes grew wide and she raised her hands in alarm.

"Please don't cry out!" Leonardo pleaded. He spread his empty palms in an appeasing gesture.

"What are you doing here?" Lucrezia exclaimed. "You are both fugitives."

"But we are not murderers," said Leonardo. "As I told you at the Duomo, we are innocent."

Fresina nodded vehemently. "What he says is true, mistress."

Lucrezia gripped the back of the divan, her nails digging into the fabric. "Where is Lorenzo?"

"He is safe," said Leonardo. "He protected us from harm so the truth could be made known. He would have given anything to be here in my place, but he would never have made it this far without being recognised. And what matters to him most of all is that you should be rescued."

"Rescued?" Lucrezia's eyelids fluttered uncertainly. "You can't believe I am in any danger here."

Fresina made a disgusted noise at the back of her throat. "Of course you are in danger. The whole city goes to war."

"If Neroni is pushed to the wall, you may be the last card he has left to play against the Medici," said Leonardo.

Lucrezia wrung her fingers. "I grant you Neroni is

unscrupulous, but I am under Luca Pitti's protection and he has always been a man of honour."

"Honour and ambition often go together," said Leonardo, "and one can corrupt the other. Have you tried to leave the palace?"

Lucrezia's long eyelashes drooped. "I am never left alone. Even when I stroll in the grounds, there are always soldiers close by, keeping me in sight. I suppose I knew all along that I could not leave."

"Well, now you must," said Leonardo. He brought out the brooch Lorenzo had given him and offered it to her. "Lorenzo wanted me to give this to you, as a token."

Lucrezia took it tentatively from his hand, as though it might burn her fingers. "Yes, it was not so long ago that I gave this to him." The faintest shadow of a smile touched her lips. "We were going to a masked ball, and I gave him this brooch so that no matter what costume or disguise he wore, I would know it was him."

"He needs you now," said Leonardo. "Neroni intends to use you as a hostage to bend Lorenzo to his will. That is why you must come away with us now."

Lucrezia seemed to take strength from the brooch. As she pinned it to the front of her dress, she straightened her back and raised her head. "What do you want me to do?"

"You must act as though you are still an honoured guest and we are two servants sent to attend you," said Leonardo.

Darting ahead of them, Fresina opened the door a crack and peeked out. "The way is clear."

They left the room and headed down the passage.

"Once we are outside, I will give you this cloak and hood to hide your face until we reach our wagon," Leonardo explained. "We can conceal you in there and take you to safety."

"You make it sound very easy," said Lucrezia, a glint of her usual humour in her eye.

"Good. That's exactly what I'm trying to do."

A brief but dazzling smile flitted across Lucrezia's face. "Every time I meet you I end up playing some sort of game. I am beginning to wonder if I shall ever cease being a party to your tricks."

"This is the last one, I promise," said Leonardo, returning her smile.

They hurried down a staircase that gave access to a spacious gallery. They slowed to a sedate pace at the sight of a band of brightly garbed men and women coming towards them, laughing and joking. The revellers bowed their heads to Lucrezia as they passed and one of them raised his cup to her in amiable salute.

At the far end of the gallery they passed through an arch. Another passage loomed and the three fugitives quickened their pace.

"So you have not overheard Neroni or Pitti say anything about their plot to bring down the Medici?" Leonardo asked Lucrezia.

"No, the first I heard of it was from you."

"Have they mentioned the artist Silvestro or a machine he built for them?"

Lucrezia shook her head. "I have no idea what you're talking about."

Leonardo felt his heart sink. He had been hoping against hope that Lucrezia would provide him with some clue that would complete the puzzle. They took another staircase down to ground level and Leonardo paused to check his bearings.

"There is a small back door intended for bringing firewood into the palace," he said. "We should be able to sneak out that way and then get back to the wagon under cover of darkness."

They passed along a row of marble statuettes, each perched on its own slender plinth. They had not gone far when they were halted by the sound of voices from the corner ahead.

"Place guards at all the exits and stairways," they heard Neroni order, "and bring more men in to carry out a search!"

"Are you sure you're not overreacting, my friend?" said Luca Pitti.

"Why do you think anyone would tell a false story of your being ill unless they wanted to get Lucrezia alone?" Neroni retorted. "And why would they want that unless they mean to spirit her away?"

Lucrezia bit on her finger to cut off a scream. Leonardo looked round for a hiding place, but there was none.

The next instant Neroni and Pitti rounded the corner with three soldiers behind. They pulled up short at the sight of Leonardo and the two girls.

"Guards! Guards!" yelled Pitti, his voice echoing down the passageways.

"Seize them!" Neroni commanded.

The three soldiers charged forward. Before Leonardo could intervene, Fresina snatched one of the statuettes from its plinth. It was a figure dressed in a winged helmet with winged sandals on its feet. Holding it by its legs she whipped it back and forth like a club. The foremost soldier leapt aside to avoid a crack across the face.

"No, you silly child!" Pitti exclaimed in horror. "That

statue of Mercury is irreplaceable!"

"Run!" Fresina yelled, still flailing the priceless statue at the attackers.

Leonardo froze, shamed by the prospect of leaving Fresina behind. But he realised that if he allowed them all to be captured, he would be letting her courage go to waste. He grabbed Lucrezia by the hand and pulled her after him towards the stairway.

"Careful, you fools!" they heard Pitti shout at his men. "I'll have the hide of any man who so much as chips that statue."

"Come one step nearer and I will smash it against the wall!" Fresina threatened.

"We can't just leave Fresina behind," Lucrezia gasped.

"We have to trust to her wits," said Leonardo, "and hope she can get away."

He bounded up the steps two at a time, hauling the girl up after him.

"What about us?" panted Lucrezia. "How can we possibly escape?"

Leonardo said nothing. His mind raced along the passages of the Pitti Palace ahead of them, retracing the detailed lines of Filippo's plans in a desperate search for escape. He had heard Pitti and Neroni order the doors guarded, so how were they to get out?

They cleared the last step, returning to the middle floor of the palace. Leonardo was still ransacking his memory for an exit. All he could recall were galleries, passages, stairways, all of them leading to dead ends or going further up and further away from freedom.

Then his mind stretched beyond the palace walls and he found what he was looking for.

"Come on!" he exclaimed in a whoop of triumph. "There is a way out of the maze."

He dashed along the passage with Lucrezia on his heels. Behind them came the thunder of running feet.

"Forget the slave girl!" came Neroni's voice. "Catch Lucrezia and that cursed boy!"

Rapid footsteps came pounding up the stairway.

"Where are we going?" Lucrezia asked as they twisted this way and that through the intersecting corridors. They were entering an ill-lit, unfinished area of the palace.

"Down here," panted Leonardo, "is a window that overlooks the roof of the stable. It's only a drop of a few feet. From there we can climb down to the ground."

They reached the end of a bare-walled passage that was choked with workmen's clutter. Side-stepping a sack of plaster powder, Leonardo threw open a door and waved Lucrezia inside.

The girl tumbled into the room and fell to her knees, panting.

Leonardo closed the door quietly and looked around the gloomy chamber. It was lit only by a pale shaft of moonlight filtering wanly through the high, arched window.

The footsteps of Pitti's soldiers could be heard clearly now amid the banging of doors. "Search every room!" an officer commanded, his voice reverberating down the corridor.

Leonardo dashed to the window and threw it wide open. He caught his breath and gaped in sudden horror.

Lucrezia joined him. "What is it?" she asked.

Then she looked down and gasped. There was only a sheer wall plunging down into the gloom below.

"You said the stable roof would be here," said Lucrezia in a brittle, frightened voice. "You said we could climb down."

"It was in the plans," groaned Leonardo, "*but they haven't built it yet.*"

25

The Pit

Lucrezia turned white and pressed a kerchief to her mouth to stifle a sob. "This has all been for nothing."

Leonardo stared numbly into the darkness. There were some horses out there herded into a flimsy enclosure which served in place of the unbuilt stable. Beyond gaped the quarry that had been gouged out of the hillside to provide stone for the palace. Closer, between the enclosure and the wall below, was a wagon. It was piled high with hay to feed the horses.

Leonardo's heart gave a leap. "We can still get down," he exclaimed. "We can jump to that wagon and the straw will break our fall."

Lucrezia stared at him, aghast. "No, it's as good as suicide to attempt it. We don't have wings."

In her agitation she lost her grip on her kerchief. It fell out of the window, floating downward through the night air. In spite of the danger, Leonardo felt compelled to watch it fall, counting the seconds it took to settle on the straw below. From down the corridor the sound of banging doors and barking voices grew louder.

Leonardo surveyed the prospect again with his artist's eye for distance. The wagon did look very small and it stood a good six feet from the wall, but perhaps there was a way after all.

He looked around and was gripped by a sudden inspiration. "We may not have wings," he said, "but we can have the next best thing."

He took hold of the nearest curtain and with two sharp tugs broke it free of the wooden rings that held it in place. Gathering it up in his arms, he climbed on to the window ledge.

"Come up here with me," he said. "We'll use this to break our fall."

Lucrezia stood unmoving and stared at him as if he had gone mad. "What are you talking about?"

"Didn't you see how your kerchief fell?" Leonardo

asked. "It fell slowly. Why? Because it was gathering air under it, just like a bird's wings. This curtain will slow our fall in the same way."

"Are you mad?" Lucrezia asked disbelievingly.

"When you looked at the portrait I painted, you said no one had ever seen you so truly," Leonardo reminded her. "When you looked at me I had the same feeling. Look now and see if I am telling the truth."

Slowly Lucrezia met his gaze and their eyes locked. She took a hesitant step closer and accepted his outstretched hand to climb up on to the ledge beside him.

"Take these two corners," Leonardo said, offering her one end of the curtain. "Wrap the fabric around your wrists so it doesn't come loose."

The girl followed his instructions and Leonardo took a firm grip on the other two corners. Lucrezia looked into his face then down at the wagon below. "I don't know if I have the courage," she said.

Leonardo did his best to sound calm. "Have you ever jumped off a high rock into a river?"

"No, never."

"Well, I have, and believe me, it's a lot worse than this."

When I did that, Leonardo recalled, *I nearly drowned.* The memory made him suddenly dizzy.

"Are you ready?" he asked.

"I won't ever be ready," said Lucrezia. "Just tell me when to jump."

"When we go, leap as far as you can then let your body go loose. And don't let go of the curtain." He shook the fabric out so that it billowed like a sail.

They heard a door crash open in the adjacent room. Heavy boots stamped across the bare wooden floor. "Nothing here," a gruff voice reported. "Let's move on."

"When I say 'now'," said Leonardo. He heard a soft whisper coming from Lucrezia's lips. It was a prayer, a prayer to Our Lady and all the angels.

Footsteps were approaching the door directly behind them. Leonardo's throat was so dry the word came out as a croak. "*Now.*"

They flung themselves off the ledge. The curtain swelled above them like a canopy then pulled taut, painfully wrenching their outstretched arms. Leonardo was sure his heart must have stopped for he felt for an instant as though he were suspended in a supernatural stillness. There was no sound, no motion, just the uncanny sensation of being held aloft.

Then they dropped, the curtain snapping and twisting overhead, down and down into the waiting straw. The material slipped from Leonardo's grasp and he sank into a rough tangle of darkness. It was like plunging again into the River Arno, the current sucking him under as it had once before.

He gasped and struggled, as though he were fighting his way up from a muddy river bed. Then his head broke clear of the straw and he drank in the clear, blessed air.

He was alive, unhurt and free. A breathy laugh sounded in his ears like the tinkling of a bell. Lucrezia flung an arm around his neck and pressed her cheek against his. "Leonardo, we made it!" she exclaimed joyfully.

Leonardo found himself grinning crazily. "Good. Now let's get out of here."

He rolled out of the wagon and landed nimbly on his feet. He reached up and lifted Lucrezia down. "If we could only find a bridle, we could ride out of here on one of those horses," he said.

"I'm afraid there isn't going to be time for that," rasped a vengeful voice.

Leonardo thrust Lucrezia behind him as Rodrigo stepped out of a shadowy doorway. The Spaniard drew a short sword from its sheath. The moonlight glinted along the razor-sharp edge. The top of the blade was as wide as a man's hand and tapered down to a point as sharp as a needle's.

"Knowing how *elusive* you can be," he hissed, "I thought it best to cut off any possible escape route."

A voice rang out from a window overhead, the one from which they had just leapt. "Who's that down there?"

Rodrigo looked up. "The ones you are chasing, Lucrezia and the boy!" he called back.

Leonardo seized his chance. He pushed Lucrezia ahead of him and cried, "Go!"

This time Lucrezia did not hesitate. Together they bolted away from the lights of the palace towards the blackness of the quarry.

Rodrigo let out a dry laugh and started after them.

Keeping Lucrezia ahead of him, Leonardo wove through mounds of gravelly debris and crude lumps of rock waiting to be hewn into shape. There were buckets and hoists scattered about the place, and picks and shovels laid aside by the workmen at the end of the day. To trip on any of them would mean death.

Leonardo could hear Rodrigo closing in behind but dared not pause to look round. He could tell that Lucrezia's heavy dress was impeding her legs and she was getting short of breath. They were almost at the edge of the quarry when she stumbled and fell.

Leonardo dropped to one knee beside her. He saw that

her hands had been cut on the stony ground and there were tears in her eyes. Before he could help her up, a boot thudded painfully into his shoulder and pitched him on to his back.

Rodrigo stood over him, the point of the sword poised over his chest. His lip curled in a cruel sneer. "If you have any sense at all, boy, you will keep still and let me kill you quickly."

Leonardo tensed in anticipation of the fatal thrust. Just then a shrill voice split the air with a torrent of Circassian curses. Fresina jumped from behind a mound of rubble and tossed a double handful of dirt right into the Spaniard's eyes.

Rodrigo snarled and staggered back. With his free hand, he rubbed at his stinging eyes while slashing the air in front of him with his sword. Leonardo rolled to his feet. Snatching up a nearby shovel, he caught Fresina's eye.

"Get Lucrezia away!" he told her.

Fresina was still cursing in her native tongue as she hauled her mistress to her feet. As the two girls ran off towards the trees, Leonardo braced himself to meet Rodrigo.

Shaking the last of the grit from his eyes, the Spaniard lashed out with his sword. Leonardo jumped back, holding the shovel protectively in front of him.

Rodrigo grinned maliciously, exposing his sharp, white teeth. "Have you had any military training, boy? No, I didn't think so. You Florentines are all too soft for soldiering. That is why you hire foreigners like me to fight your battles for you."

Suddenly, he lunged. Leonardo made a clumsy effort to block the blow, but the steel point ripped his hose and tore a cut across his thigh. He bit his lip and pulled away, blood trickling down his leg.

Rodrigo whipped his sword this way and that so it danced in the air like the head of a poisonous snake. "Where next, eh? The arm or the throat? Suppose I slice open your belly and leave you here with your guts spilling out?"

Leonardo's leg burned and a wave of nausea swept over him. Desperately he pushed aside his fear as he had done on the window ledge and focused on the deadly struggle that lay before him. He was outmatched in both skill and weaponry. His only chance was to be more clear-headed than his enemy. He could not make Rodrigo afraid, but he could cloud his mind with anger.

"You brag of what a great soldier you are, but how did you fare as a sailor?" Leonardo asked in a mocking tone. "Did you enjoy your voyage?"

Rodrigo clenched his teeth.

"How did you enjoy Pisa?" Leonardo pressed him. "Did you visit the famous tower?"

The whole time his head was growing clearer, his eyes alert for any opening he could use.

"By Christ's wounds, you dog, I'll pay you a cut for every one of your taunts!" Rodrigo roared.

A tensing of the right shoulder gave warning of the Spaniard's next attack. Ducking away, Leonardo evaded a vicious slash that would have cut his throat wide open. He swung the shovel, struck a glancing blow off his enemy's ribs, then retreated as fast as he could.

Rodrigo's eyes blazed like coals in a furnace. A feral snarl rattled in his throat, and he launched a flurry of ill-aimed blows at the boy who had so frustrated him.

Leonardo dodged this way and that, using his clumsy weapon to fend off the Spaniard's furious blade. Their battle took them to within a few paces of the quarry's edge, where the blackness yawned like a vast, empty pool. Rodrigo pressed his attack, his movements becoming wilder as his anger possessed him.

Leonardo wondered if the man was blind to the danger that lay so close. Out of the corner of his eye, he saw that Lucrezia and Fresina had almost reached the shelter of the trees. Soon they would be safe and all the danger would be worthwhile.

Through the haze of his rage, Rodrigo spotted them too.

"I have no more time to waste with you, boy," he spat. "I must be after my prey."

Just as Leonardo's keen eyes could pick out every movement of a bird in flight, so he was now attuned to every twitch of Rodrigo's body. To his amazement, the Spaniard lowered his sword. Then his left eye narrowed, just as it had at Anchiano when a throwing knife had sprung into his hand.

Reacting by sheer instinct, Leonardo whipped the shovel head up to cover his breast. The steel point intended for his heart clanged against the metal and dropped harmlessly to the ground.

Before the Spaniard could recover, Leonardo charged him, driving the shovel hard into his enemy's belly. Rodrigo reeled back, winded, and raised his sword to strike.

But there was only empty air under his feet. Limbs flailing wildly, the sword flying from his grasp, he plummeted down the sheer slope. The jagged rocks ripped his tunic and raked his body. An anguished cry burst from his throat as the darkness of the pit swallowed him up.

For a few moments there was silence. Leonardo stood

swaying with exhaustion, barely able to take in his victory.

Then there came a great roar from behind him. He turned wearily to see a mob of men with torches and swords running towards him from the palace. Neroni was at their head, urging them on with blood-curdling threats.

Leonardo tried to flee, but the wound in his thigh sent a shock of pain through his body. The shovel slipped from his numbed fingers and he crumpled to his knees.

26

THE MACHINERY OF DEATH

Leonardo waited resignedly for violent hands to seize him and drag him off to the palace. *At least we rescued Lucrezia,* he thought. It was some consolation to know that he had repaid his debt to Lorenzo.

Unexpectedly his ears were filled with the thunder of hooves. As he looked up, a dozen horses burst out of the trees and came streaming past him, their riders armed with lances and swords. At the sight of them, Neroni's men, all on foot, reared back as if a wall of fire had erupted from the earth right in front of them.

Neroni brandished his sword in futile rage when

he saw Lorenzo de' Medici in command of the rescue party. "This will not help you, Lorenzo!" he yelled. "Mark my words – you will be sorry you did not remain at home!"

Leonardo heard a voice close by. "Come on, Leonardo," it urged. "This is no time to dawdle."

It was Sandro peering down at him from the saddle of a grey mare. He looked far from secure and was clinging tightly to the pommel. In his left hand he held the reins of a second horse, the very one Leonardo had ridden from Careggi. The animal seemed to recognise him and bent down to nuzzle his face.

Leonardo grabbed the stirrup to haul himself upright then climbed painfully into the saddle. "Sandro, how did you get here?"

"No time for questions," said Sandro. "Let's get out of here."

They wheeled about and headed for the trees. As soon as they were out of danger, Lorenzo turned his horsemen around and galloped after them, leaving Neroni fuming in their dust.

In a clearing beyond the trees, Lucrezia waited on horseback with two mounted attendants guarding her.

"Where's Fresina?" Leonardo asked, reining in.

"Here!" The slave girl appeared out of the shadows and stood by her mistress.

"How did you get out of the palace?" Leonardo asked.

"Everybody was running around thinking they were under attack," Fresina laughed. "Nobody paid attention to a small, unarmed girl."

Sandro clambered down from his horse and examined Leonardo's leg. "That's an ugly wound," he said, unwrapping a kerchief from around his neck. He wrapped the material around the wound and knotted it tightly. "This will have to do until we can get to a physician."

"I see you've picked up a thing or two from your mother," said Leonardo.

"Just be glad I don't have any nettles," Sandro chuckled as he got back in the saddle.

Lorenzo pulled up beside them, his horse rearing and beating the air with its front hooves. He settled the animal and moved close to Lucrezia.

A teardrop glinted on the girl's cheek. "Lorenzo, they told me nothing of what was happening in the city. I hardly dared hope that…"

Lorenzo silenced her by leaning forward and brushing her lips with a feather-light kiss. He gently tapped the jewelled brooch that was pinned to her dress. "I told you when you gave me this that we would always find each other, no matter what."

He turned to Leonardo. "Where other men would have shunned the danger, you have succeeded," he said. "You have my gratitude."

"And you have mine for showing up when you did," said Leonardo. "I thought you were forbidden to come here."

"Shortly before supper I retired to my rooms with an upset stomach," said Lorenzo with a grin. "Who should I meet on the way, but these good friends of mine who persuaded me that a ride in the fresh air would restore my health." He gestured at his companions, who all laughed good-naturedly at his joke. "By a lucky coincidence our ride took us to the Oltrarno, just in time to get you out of your difficulties."

"We'd best be off before Neroni gives chase," Bartolomeo's gruff voice warned.

Lucrezia offered a hand to Fresina and pulled her up on to the saddle behind her. The girl wrapped her arms around her mistress's waist and the party set off towards the river.

When they reached the Ponte alle Grazia, they saw Neroni's guards bound and gagged with a pair of Medici soldiers keeping watch over them. Lorenzo led everyone to the far side of the river then reined in.

"Neroni may try to pursue," he told Leonardo and Sandro. "I will stay here with my men and hold the bridge secure while you see the ladies safely back to my father's house."

Leonardo felt honoured by Lorenzo's trust and led the way through the dark streets with Sandro riding at his side. Lucrezia and Fresina followed a few paces behind.

Lucrezia was safe now, but Leonardo was still uneasy. He remained convinced something was missing, something as central to Neroni's plot as the vital cog Silvestro had left out of his diagram.

Despite the pain and fatigue, his mind was racing once again. Piero's unvarying routine, Silvestro's carefully constructed device... and Fresina, keeping Neroni at bay with a piece of statuary. Time, a spring – and a god!

Leonardo jolted as if he had been struck by a thunderbolt. All the clues he had been chasing for days were falling into place like the workings of a clock. He gasped aloud.

"What is it, Leonardo?" asked Sandro. "What's wrong?"

"Everything is wrong!" Leonardo exclaimed. "The burglars at the Medici house, they weren't stealing something, they were *replacing* something."

"Replacing what?"

"It's so obvious. Don't you see? The symbols on the back of Silvestro's drawing aren't planets, they're *gods.* What Fresina heard them say was that Piero would be struck down by the hand of a god. One of the bronze statues in the Medici dining hall has been replaced with a duplicate."

"What on earth for?"

"To kill Piero de' Medici while he's at supper, of course. To fire a missile and kill him!"

Sandro stared back at him blankly. "Are you sure that is its purpose?"

"Yes, and for the first time I'm sure of my purpose too," said Leonardo. "To understand all this, and by understanding save a life – perhaps even a city." He gave his mount a kick and started it forward.

"Not so fast, Leonardo," Sandro called after him. "This horse has little respect for my directions."

Leonardo raced off through the dark streets and galloped into the Via Larga. The men patrolling there were taken by surprise as he flew past them towards the Medici house. He pulled back on the reins and the horse reared up before the closed gate, snorting furiously.

"Let me in!" Leonardo shouted. "I have an urgent message for Ser Piero!"

Sandro caught up as the guards were opening the gate and they rode together into the courtyard. Leonardo slipped down from the saddle, his injured leg almost giving way beneath him as he touched the ground.

Sandro dismounted laboriously and took his friend's arm to support him. One of the Medici servants approached with a concerned frown.

"Let me fetch a physician," he offered.

"No time for that," said Leonardo. "I must see Piero de' Medici at once."

"Impossible," said the servant. "He is at his supper and must not be disturbed for any reason. There are guards on the door with strict orders to that effect."

Leonardo did not waste time arguing. Pulling away from Sandro, he barged into the house and ran as fast as he could down the corridors. The wound Rodrigo had inflicted on him blazed like a fire in his leg and he could feel blood seeping through the makeshift bandage, but desperation drove him on. He raced ahead like a man leaping through flames to escape a burning building while Sandro struggled to catch up.

"Leonardo, stop!" Sandro pleaded. "You're going to

bleed to death at this rate."

They turned a corner and saw the door to the dining hall guarded by two armed men. At the sight of the intruders the guards lowered their spears and fixed the intruders with a menacing grimace. The two young artists skidded to a halt.

"They're not going to let us past," hissed Leonardo. "Maybe if you talk to them, Sandro, distract them..."

Sandro swallowed hard, like a man who has just made a fearful decision. "No, Leonardo, this time I'm going to do things your way." His jaw was set in a determined grimace Leonardo had never seen on his friend's face before.

"What do you mean?"

"I'm going to charge in without thinking," said Sandro. "It's like a game of football. I'll lead the way and you follow with the ball. If you can be a lion, so can I."

With that, he lowered his head and barrelled forward. The guards were so astonished they hadn't time to react before Sandro dived under the spearpoints and clipped their legs out from under them. All three of them crashed to the floor, Sandro doing his best to pin the guards down.

Leonardo sprinted after, jumping over the struggling trio and slamming through the door. Guests jumped up from their places at table. Several men drew their swords and cried out in alarm. Only Piero de' Medici remained calm, barely turning his head to see what the uproar was about.

Leonardo paid no attention. All he saw were the three bronze statues perched upon their marble pedestals. He had noticed them before without realising their significance. On one side, Mars the god of war, on the other, Venus the goddess of love, and in the centre, Jupiter the king of the gods.

And in Jupiter's upraised right hand – as sharp and deadly as an arrow – was a thunderbolt, a jagged missile of bronze.

Leonardo bounded across the room. Two servants moved to intercept him, but they were not quick enough. Every step was a jarring jolt of agony, but Leonardo's ever acute ears detected the sound of the mechanism concealed inside the bronze Jupiter finishing its cycle.

A dropping weight, the whirr of spinning cogs.

Leonardo threw himself onward at full stretch. Even as the spring-loaded arm snapped forward, his fingertips struck the pedestal. The pedestal rocked and Jupiter tilted backwards just as the thunderbolt shot from his bronze fingers.

Like a dart from a crossbow the missile streaked through the air. With a thud it pierced the wooden panel two feet above Piero de' Medici's head, missing the heart that had been its intricately calculated target.

Leonardo sprawled flat out on the floor, his strength exhausted. As pandemonium erupted all around him, his eyes closed and blackness engulfed him. He was falling endlessly through a dark and empty sky. He was falling, but he was not afraid, for at his back he could feel the beating of wings.

27

THE AGE OF WONDERS

"Leonardo, you're up at last!" Sandro exclaimed as he entered the chamber.

Leonardo was making his way gingerly around the bed in a series of small, careful steps. "Yes, the Medici family physicians say I can leave today. But don't tell your brother. He'll have me back on the football field before I can run."

Sandro rubbed his wrist. "Yes," he agreed wryly, "I think we can both do with a break from that."

Piero de' Medici had insisted that Leonardo stay at their town house while he recuperated from his wound. It was two days since the escape from the Pitti Palace and much had happened in that short time.

With Lucrezia free and his father safe from harm, Lorenzo had summoned a gathering of all the citizens of Florence and personally supervised the election of the new Signoria. Neroni, seeing the tide of events going against him, had fled the city with his henchmen. Luca Pitti came to beg forgiveness of Piero. He denied any knowledge of the murder plot and claimed the whole business was a dreadful misunderstanding. Today, the fate of the conspirators was to be decided.

Sandro spotted a bowl of fruit on the bedside table and helped himself to a juicy apple. "I've just come from the meeting of the Signoria," he reported. "They granted a pardon to Luca Pitti, at Piero de' Medici's request, but he will never hold public office again."

"What about Neroni?"

"He was unanimously sentenced to death, but Piero exercised his influence again to have the sentence commuted to exile."

"I suppose he still doesn't want anyone's blood on his hands, not even that of his worst enemy," said Leonardo. "Has there been any sign of Rodrigo?"

Sandro shook his head. "I assume he survived the fall and fled along with Neroni."

In spite of everything the Spaniard had done, Leonardo was relieved. Like Piero, he had no desire to be responsible for anyone's death.

"All of this is good," he said, "but none of it explains why you're looking so pleased with yourself."

"Well, now that all these madcap adventures are done, I have to get back to my proper work," said Sandro. He paused to take a bite of the apple. "First I have to paint a fresh portrait of Lucrezia to replace the one that was damaged. Then Piero wants me to do a special painting to commemorate their escape from Neroni's plot."

"And so begins the career of the artist Alessandro Botticelli!" Leonardo declared grandly.

Sandro took a mock bow. "There would be only a disaster to commemorate if not for your quick thinking."

"Quick thinking?" Leonardo sank down on the edge of the bed and absently stroked his bandaged thigh. "I should have seen it long before. Silvestro was an apprentice of Donatello, who made all three of those Roman gods. Silvestro probably assisted in casting the bronze Jupiter, which made it easy for him to fashion a copy."

"I don't think Piero will feel any less grateful for the

delay," said Sandro. "I'm sure he's offered to reward you handsomely."

"The subject has come up," Leonardo responded evasively.

"Well, what did you ask for? A post in his household? Gold? Jewels? A villa in the country?"

"You know what my price is, Sandro," Leonardo replied. "I asked him to buy me a bird."

"A bird?" Sandro was incredulous.

As if in response to their words, Fresina came flying excitedly through the door. She pulled up short when she saw Sandro was there.

"Fresina, what are you doing here?" Sandro asked.

"My master sent me," the girl replied. She walked up to Leonardo and tapped a finger on his chest. "My *old* master. He said that you bought me from him."

Leonardo shook his head. "It was Piero de' Medici who bought you. He gave you to me as a gift."

Fresina shrugged. "Either way, I am your slave now."

"Not at all," said Leonardo. "I've already set you free. The papers have all been signed."

Fresina blinked. "But why would you do that?"

Leonardo stood up. "Because I want to see you fly," he answered simply.

Fresina's mouth opened, but no sound came out. Leonardo couldn't help feeling a glow of satisfaction at seeing her speechless at last.

"Lucrezia would have granted you your freedom, if that were within her power," he said, "but only her father had the authority to do that."

Fresina still looked more confused than happy. "I should go back to the Torre Donati," she said, touching a hand to her brow, "to pack my things, such as they are."

"I think you'll find Lucrezia has added a purse of florins to your belongings," said Leonardo, "as a token of her gratitude."

Fresina turned to leave, then stopped short. "But where am I to go? I may be free but now I have no home."

"Didn't my mother tell you she would always have a place for you?" Leonardo reminded her.

Fresina nodded slowly.

"I'm sure you can stay with her as long as you like."

"It is a good place," said Fresina, "with brave people. But they are your family, not mine."

"Go in my place then," Leonardo encouraged her, "and live the life I might have had, if things had been different. I promise I'll come and visit."

For a moment silence hung between them. Then the girl

threw her arms around his neck and hugged him close. Leonardo could feel her heart beating excitedly against his chest and he felt a share of her joy ignite within him, like a flame being passed from one candle to another. When she pulled away there was a tear in her eye.

"Thank you, Leonardo," she said, "for all that you have done."

"I thought slaves didn't feel gratitude," said Leonardo.

"They don't," said Fresina with a broad smile. "But I am free now and I can feel anything I want."

She made to leave, pausing for a moment in the doorway. "Don't forget you promised to visit," she said, wagging a finger at Leonardo. "You know what the Brawler will do to you if you break your word."

Leonardo raised his hands in surrender. "I swear you will see me on the next feast day," he said. "Tell my mother to set a place for me."

Fresina gave a last grin then skipped away, closing the door behind her.

"She's a remarkable girl," Sandro said admiringly. "One day I really would like to use her as a model in one of my paintings."

"A model for what?" Leonardo asked. "Not a saint, I hope!"

"No, nothing as tame as that," Sandro laughed. "I shall paint her as a pagan goddess. Yes, that's it – the goddess of springtime."

"Fresina has her home now," said Leonardo, "and it's time I returned to mine."

"What? Are you going back to Anchiano?" Sandro asked in surprise.

"No, I've been back to Anchiano and it was there I learned the truth," said Leonardo.

Sandro made a puzzled noise.

"It was my father who said it," Leonardo explained, "without even knowing how true his words were. He said I belonged with Andrea del Verrocchio. My father may have his plans for me, Caterina my mother may love me, and Piero de' Medici may be grateful to me. But only Maestro Andrea expects me to understand everything I see, and in doing that to achieve greatness. That's worth a few years of hard work."

"Greatness, eh?" Sandro peered at him dubiously. "I'm trying to see it, but it must be hidden very deeply."

Leonardo plucked up a cushion and took a swing with it. Sandro chuckled as he dodged the blow.

"All right, Sandro," Leonardo laughed, "I'm sure you're going to be a great man as well."

"You know," Sandro said, suddenly thoughtful, "at that party Lorenzo took me to at Alberti's house, there was a lot of talk about what an age of wonders we live in. They were saying that art, science and literature have all been reborn, right here in Florence, that the world has seen nothing like it since before the fall of Rome."

"Well, if this is an age of wonders," said Leonardo, "then perhaps anything we can imagine is possible." He turned to gaze out of the window at the clouds drifting across the sky. "Perhaps one day a man might even learn to fly."

Afterword

More than 500 years ago Leonardo da Vinci drew up plans for aeroplanes, helicopters, parachutes, submarines and diving suits. He made a detailed study of human anatomy – especially the workings of the eye – and experimented with the properties of light. And he was responsible for some of the most famous works of art ever created, including the *Mona Lisa.*

We know the details of his birth and family background from official records of the time and we know the genius he became. But in all the hundreds of pages of his notebooks Leonardo tells us almost nothing about his early years. We know of his fascination with flight and the destructive power of water, of his youthful vanity and his love of animals. But what inspired him to become a legend is a question only our imaginations can answer.

We do know that Leonardo was an apprentice in the workshop of Andrea del Verrocchio for just over ten years and that he probably arrived there in 1466. In that same year there was a conspiracy to overthrow the Medici family, the rulers of Florence. It is against this background that I have imagined my tale of the young Leonardo.

The period of history we know as the Renaissance was marked by a rediscovery of the writings, science and philosophy of the ancient Greeks and Romans. Many brilliant people appeared at this time and it seemed to them that there was no limit to what human beings could accomplish. Nowhere was this more evident than in the city of Florence in northern Italy, which produced more than its fair share of remarkable individuals.

Fresina, Rodrigo and Silvestro are entirely my invention. All the other major characters in the story were real people. Lorenzo de' Medici saved his father from Neroni's ambush just as described here. Luca Pitti did base his palace on designs originally submitted to the Medici, and Lucrezia Donati really was regarded as the most beautiful woman in Florence.

Readers might be interested to know what happened to some of these people after the events of this book.

Marriage for the leading families of Florence was a matter of duty rather than romance. Lorenzo de' Medici was married to Clarice Orsini, the daughter of a powerful Roman family, in order to strengthen the Medici business interests in that city. Lucrezia married a wealthy merchant named Pietro Ardinghelli.

Lorenzo succeeded his father as ruler of Florence in 1469. As he himself had predicted, his health suffered as a result of his responsibilities and he died at the age of forty-three. Under his rule, however, the city flourished as never before. He was the patron of Botticelli, Michelangelo and many other great artists and writers. He is remembered to this day as 'Lorenzo the Magnificent'.

Sandro Botticelli became one of the outstanding artists of the Renaissance. Some of his most famous paintings, such as the *Birth of Venus* and *Primavera*, were inspired by ancient mythology. In later life his work became more serious and more spiritual.

Paolo Toscanelli continued to chart the earth and sky. In

1492 his maps helped to guide Christopher Columbus on his voyage to the New World.

Diotisalvi Neroni continued to plot unsuccessfully against the Medici and finally died in exile.

Luca Pitti remained in Florence, but was shunned by his fellow citizens for the rest of his life. When he died bankrupt, the Medici took possession of his magnificent palace. Today it is one of the world's great museums of art.

For more background on *Leonardo and the Death Machine* visit the author's website: www.harris-authors.com

before they were heroes...

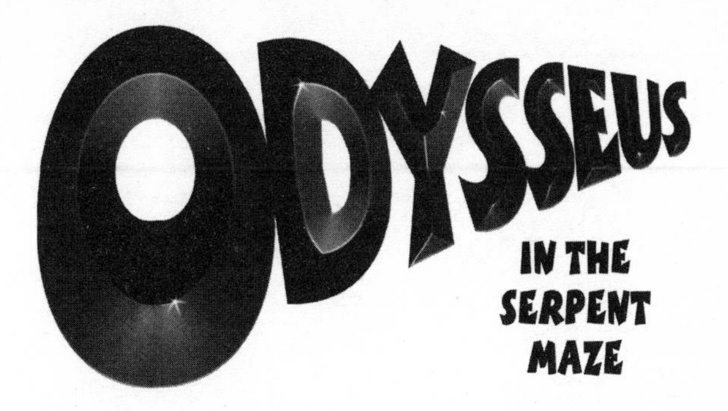

"Rescue? Is that *what you call it? Throw a rock and then run? And I bet that's as far ahead as you'd planned." Penelope made a face. "Boys! Always thinking about heroics and never about what needs to happen day to day."*

Odysseus, Prince of Ithaca, is sheltered, protected – and bored! More than anything he longs for adventure – but the Age of Heroes is over. The monsters have all been slain; the treasures have all been found; there's nothing left for Odysseus to do.

But just as Odysseus is sure that nothing interesting will *ever* happen to him, the gods step in and stir things up. And the trouble with real adventures is they never go the way you think they should. Pretty soon, the young prince discovers that the hardest part of being a hero is living long enough to tell the tale...

0-00-713414-2

www.harpercollinschildrensbooks.co.uk

HarperCollins *Children's Books*

before they were heroes...

"You expect what?" Acastus laughed. "And who are you? A peasant boy whose parents threw him out to make room for goats... If Chiron is such a wise teacher, he should have taught you to know your place, Goat Boy. Be careful what you say to princes."

Talk about attitude! Faced with this kind of reaction whenever he opens his mouth, how can Jason ever lead "his royal highness" Prince Acastus and friends on a deadly mission to save their civilisation from the Gorgon's blood – the most deadly poison in the world!

0-00-713417-7

www.harpercollinschildrensbooks.co.uk

HarperCollins *Children's Books*

3 8002 01288 5150